LOSTLANDER

BOOKS BY DEAN F. WILSON

THE CHILDREN OF TELM

The Call of Agon
The Road to Rebirth
The Chains of War

THE GREAT IRON WAR

Hopebreaker
Lifemaker
Skyshaker
Landquaker
Worldwaker
Hometaker

THE COILHUNTER CHRONICLES

Coilhunter
Rustkiller
Dustrunner
Lostlander
Sixshooter
Deadwalker

HIBERNIAN HOLLOWS

Hibernian Blood
Hibernian Charm

A COILHUNTER CHRONICLES NOVEL

LOSTLANDER

DEAN F. WILSON

Cover illustration by Duy Phan

First Edition 2019

ISBN 978-1-909356-23-8

Published by Dioscuri Press
Dublin, Ireland

www.dioscuripress.com
enquiries@dioscuripress.com

Welcome to the Wild North

CONTENTS

Chapter

Chapter One

LOST

The Coilhunter awoke in the desert. That wasn't the strange part. The desert went on for miles. If you didn't wake there, chances are you were dead. He'd gotten to know those grains, gotten to make a temporary ally of the wind and a permanent enemy of the sun. Yet here, things were different. The grains were different, a little darker than before. The caress of the wind was different too. This was a part of the Wild North he'd never been to, and he had no memory of how he got there.

He tried to stand, but his legs buckled. So, he just sat there for a moment, gathering his thoughts together. He had a dozen questions fighting to the front, and not a single answer. He had the so-called anaesthesia of the mind. He was lucky he even remembered who he was, that he knew his name was Nathaniel Osley Xander, that he knew he was Nox. But that memory brought back other, painful ones— yet nothing of this place.

"Well, old boy," he rasped. "Seems you're lost." The grit of his voice was only matched by the grit in his eyes, sandpapering his vision. The sand had a way of getting everywhere. Normally he got across it in his trusty monowheel, but he couldn't see the vehicle nearby. He was alone. That was how it usually was, but now he felt it more than ever. Something was off.

He sipped from his water canister. The liquid almost dried on his tongue before it had a chance to waterfall down his throat. It was amazing what a few drops could do, how it could bring you back from the brink, how it could work its magic on your body and give you a little clarity of mind. But there could've been a lake there, and he'd have still not known where he was. Why, if there was a lake there, then he sure as hell wasn't anywhere he'd been before.

The water did one thing though: as he swamped it down, it made him aware of something around his neck. He tugged at it with his gloved fingers, feeling a metal collar. It was thick, with many notches and ridges. And it was tight. Tight enough to dig into his adam's apple. Tight enough to make him feel each and every gulp.

There was no obvious way to remove it, not even when Nox took a screwdriver from the small box of tools on his belt and shoved it between the metal and flesh. The collar didn't bend or budge. All he did was leave a red mark on his throat, just another one to join the sun's lashes.

He cast the screwdriver away in frustration, then realised his error and scrambled to find it again. The sand would bury that if he wasn't looking, like it'd bury him if he wasn't moving. Right now all he could do was sit or crawl, and ponder about this unusual predicament. The feeling was starting to return to his legs, but it didn't return quick. Night would return quicker, and while it was often better than day, it was only better if you could start a fire. Nox hated the fire, and hated more that he needed it. To him, it was like a slave needing the whip. That just reminded him of the collar again, of the feeling like he wasn't quite a man now, but a dog—and a stray one at that.

"Keep it together, Nox," he told himself. Of course, he couldn't help but think that talking to himself meant he wasn't keeping it together at all. He'd faced worse things than this before. He'd faced bigger threats. Yet he couldn't shake a fear in his gut, the kind of fear he usually instilled in others, in the conmen and criminals of the Wild North.

He looked for clues in the land around him, that ever-shifting, ever-unreliable land. It was as bad as the fire and the sun. The sooner you learned that the land didn't like you, the better. But then, if the land stood on you, wouldn't you be unhappy? Maybe the folk that walked it were just another shackle, just another collar made of flesh.

There were no answers in the grains, not the subtle kind, and definitely not the kind some tribesfolk claimed to see, the so-called grainreading, where the sand formed itself into shapes and spelled out letters. If it'd do that for him, you can damn well bet that it wouldn't spell anything nice.

"Try to remember," he said. He racked his brain for the pieces the land wouldn't give him. He stared down the alleys of the mind, hoping to find something he'd missed. It was all a haze, like the shimmer on the horizon, which masked the endless, rolling dunes. He could try to journey out there, but there was no knowing where "there" was, not if he didn't know where "here" was either.

Then something caught in the monowheel of his mind. It jammed there, making him fixate on it. He saw a man with long, silver hair standing over him, putting the collar on. The man's eyes seemed to penetrate him, seemed to freeze every part of him, seemed to see right into his soul, where the fire burned. It was a stare that could topple plateaus, could make giants tremble. It was a look that could make a lawman like Nox feel like he was a criminal.

Still not enough, the man had said, and his voice was just as powerful, just as hypnotic. He'd said it to himself, because he paid little heed to Nox, just like he paid little heed to the dozens of other collared folk in the room. The man's frustration was palpable, contagious even. It was as if those feelings were Nox's too.

Then the question came: *Why didn't you fight?* the Coilhunter pondered. *Why did you just lie there?* He could see himself looking down past the mask on his face, past the tubes leading to the oxygen tank on his back, past the self-given sheriff's badge on his chest, down to his holstered pistols. *Why didn't he take them?* There were only more questions—and that silent, uncooperative land.

The sun tunnelled through the clouds, shining its scalding spotlight on him, but shining nothing on the events of the past few days. It was a violent world, so it was a violent sun. Maybe that was how that great yellow orb survived. But how had Nox survived? How had he escaped? A dozen more questions crowded in, like the crowd of shackled people, all staring up like him, dumbfounded. Who could have this power? Who was the owner of all these collared dogs?

Chapter Two

PAINTING A POSTER

The Coilhunter was used to unanswered questions. Normally he was doing the asking, and when the voice of his mouth didn't do it, he'd use the voice of his gun. The criminals spilled the beans more often than not, convicting those folk the lawless lands said couldn't be convicted. But there was no one here to intimidate, no one here to interrogate. He had to answer his own questions, and right now he just had a six-shooter full of blanks.

And you'd go mad that way, trying to answer the unanswerable. He'd almost gone there when he searched for the killer of his family, back five years ago. The only thing that kept him sane was the hunt for justice. It was still keeping him sane, though undoubtedly many thought he'd well and truly cracked. The things he made didn't help his image, though they helped his fight. His gizmos. His gadgets. He still had some of them strapped to his belt. It didn't make any sense why he still had them. Those were the first things you'd take if you captured him. You wouldn't try to cage the Coilhunter and keep him armed. Yet that's just what the Man with the Silver Mane did.

"I'll find you," he said to that phantom image, like he said to the shadow of his family's killer. He'd made good on that promise, and he already had a head start on this one. Why, he already had a face for the Wanted poster. It wouldn't pay in coils, sure enough, but there was another currency that sustained the Coilhunter even more: vengeance. He'd had his wage of that and more.

He struggled to his feet again, taking that first little step of the hunt. It always started small, more in the mind than the flesh. But once he knew he wouldn't topple over, he pulled up a bigger bucket of conviction from those deep, dark wells of strength buried within him.

He started off, choosing a direction and sticking with it, even though he didn't know where it'd go. He used the compass of the sun to guide him, a momentary truce with that scalding boulder in the sky. He headed south, reasoning that if he were still in the Wild North—which was just guesswork at this point—then the only way to get to the parts of it he knew, and civilisation far south, was to go in the opposite direction. But reason was a fickle thing in the desert. The land scoffed at it. The sun derided it. The wind eroded the bones of the reasonable just as easily as the irrational.

He picked up the pace as the sun dipped on his right, not stopping for food, not halting for rest. He'd slept a lot lately, it seemed. Now was the time for waking, and the time for walking. Now was the time for killing. He didn't know for certain what the Man with the Silver Mane did, but he knew it was wrong.

That was about all he knew. He knew it in his gut like he knew the Northfolk. And he could sure as hell bet this silver-haired fellow wasn't from the Wild North.

As he walked, he painted that poster in his mind a little clearer. He filled in the details around those crystal eyes, those shifting caverns of jade and sapphire. How could a man's eyes seem so different every time you stared at them? No matter. Nox wouldn't let that stop him pinning up that poster, wouldn't let it stop him etching in those damning words: *Dead or Not Alive.*

Chapter Three

PYRE

Nox kept going, until his old aches were replaced by new ones. He watched the sun die from the corner of his eye, knowing it'd be back for him soon enough. Unlike it, you never came back. The chill seized him pretty quick. Even his brisk march wasn't enough to fend off the cold. He was forced to stop and start a fire.

He assembled the dried-up desert brush he'd collected on his way south and gave it a proper funeral. The pyre warmed his body, but his soul was still cold, like it was still frozen from the Man with the Silver Mane's icicle stare. As the bristles burned, he felt a connection to that man, felt his hand around his neck, where the collar was. Yet, the closer he got to the fire, the less he felt it. He wasn't sure if that was just comfort—or something else.

The night was eerily quiet. He couldn't hear the howls of far-off coyotes, couldn't hear the hoots of owls or the screech of hawks. The only sound was the crackle of the fire, which brought to mind that *other* fire, the one that competed with the ice inside his soul.

He tried to sleep, but the night was as restless

as he was. Every time the fire burned low, he felt the darkness sneak in to smother him. He saw the watchful, crystal eyes. The only way to stamp them out, to dull their grasping stare, was to make the fire a little fiercer. He hated that the fire was even more a friend now, because it remained an enemy in his dreams.

When day broke, he found himself poking at the embers, his mind groggy. He thought maybe he whispered a name. *Emma.* Oh, how he'd whispered that so many nights before. The loneliness felt stronger now. He wasn't even sure what day it was. He hoped it wasn't Monday. That was *their* day. He couldn't journey to them if he didn't know where he was. By rights, he couldn't journey to them at all, not where they were now—not until he finished his work here, while there was still so much to clean up in the Wild North.

He ventured out, keeping that southern path, even when the sun tried to blind him as it too travelled south. He kept the brim of his hat down, fending off the glare and fighting off the periodic sandstorms. He chased the horizon, which was like a fleeing criminal. The desert shrunk as he approached a dune, but it expanded again when he clambered up. The spirits of the sand were playing accordion with his eyes. The tribesfolk had a name for that too: the silent music of the sand. Some even said it was the breathing of the earth. Well, it was no surprise that there was grit in its lungs.

Then he halted, instinctively. His hand hovered, ready to draw. A thousand practice shots, and two thousand practised kills, all narrowed down into a tingle—into a twitch. His eyes scouted the area ahead of him, mapping it out, marking the best place to run, the better place to roll. He rehearsed his routine in his mind, where he'd tumble if they came from behind him, when he'd feint, and when he'd fire.

Then he caught it, like the eagle catches its prey. His eyes settled on the body of a fallen animal far off, nestled by a cactus ridge. Maybe it had tried those desert fruit for water. Or maybe it just wanted to die in the shade. You couldn't blame the dying for clinging to a little bit of comfort.

He approached it cautiously, because his gut didn't just say caution—it screamed it loud and clear. This was the first creature, besides himself, that he'd seen out here. That had to mean something.

And it did.

When he came close enough to see, he saw it was a horse. And not just any horse. It was one he knew.

It was Old Reliable.

Chapter Four

RELIABLY DEAD

Boy, that was a sight. That old sorrel was half-dead, and the half that wasn't, well, it probably should've been. The horse lay on its side, largely unmoving. It couldn't move. It's front legs'd been gnawed off, leaving just two bloody, sand-covered stumps.

Nox stood over the steed and shook his head. "Who did this to you, boy?"

The horse made a faint whiny in response. It tried to lift its head, to look towards that familiar, grit-filled voice, but it didn't have the energy for it. Some tribesfolk said you could commune with horses, learn their language. A skill like that would've been mighty useful right now. Instead, all the Coilhunter could do was keep on shaking his head.

Nox got down on his haunches and rubbed the horse's neck. Old Reliable flinched a little. No doubt the last touch he felt was the bite. Right now, he was pretty much just waiting to die. Funny, that. Most folk didn't have to wait.

"Where's your master?" Nox asked, trying to soften his voice. He knew this was the steed of that prospector-turned-drifter Thomas Oakley, better known as Chance Oakley, for all those second chances he gave. But where was he now? Nox hadn't seen him in a good three months. He couldn't help but muse that maybe this was that start of a *bad* three months for both of them.

Nox took an eyeglass from a pouch on his belt, extended the barrel, and peered out into the distance. He hoped he'd find that grey-haired drifter, or some little dot on the horizon that might've been him. Surely he went for help. But there was no help out here. And there was no Oakley.

"Can't imagine he'd just leave you like this," Nox said. "Not him." No. See, Oakley was a friend to horses, even if he didn't speak their tongue. There was a connection there, like the one between the biker gangs and their bikes. Stronger, even. So, Oakley didn't leave willingly. The question was: why was he even out here in the first place? Was he looking for Nox? Or, was Nox looking for Oakley? Or was it all just a strange coincidence, like the puppetry of malignant gods? The only thing the Coilhunter knew for certain was the haze. The haze of the desert and the haze of his mind.

Nox gave the horse a few final, gentle strokes. "There, there," he said. "It'll be over soon." He sometimes wondered if that was true. There were folk out there who seemed pretty convinced there was an afterlife, and some of them even thought it'd be a good one. So, they requested to be buried with the things they'd need there, like food or valuables. Nox thought it best that he be buried with his guns.

Nox stood up and loosened one pistol from its holster. Old Reliable stirred from the sound. They didn't need to share a language to understand the moment, that dark, impending moment. They say there's a second sense for death, that you perk up your ear when you hear the Grim Reaper calling. Well, Nox was calling now, gun in hand, and he was grimmer still.

He aimed the pistol at Old Reliable's head. He had to put that horse out of its misery. He couldn't help but wonder if someone would find him one day like this, helpless and dying. He'd rather be reliably dead.

He cocked the hammer. Normally, he asked the criminals something now, like: *Any last words?* Oh, some of them had them alright. Nasty ones. Vulgar ones. And the gestures to go with them. The Coilhunter called that *begging the trigger*. It made it easy for him.

But this wasn't easy. As much as he knew he needed to put Old Reliable out to pasture—wherever that was, what with the desert gnawing up those pastures too—he felt a reluctance in his fingers. A reluctance to kill. Maybe it was because of what Old Reliable meant to Oakley. Maybe it was because there just wasn't any fairness in this horse, once abused, then loved, dying like this.

Whatever it was, it stopped him hitting the trigger for just long enough to hear something in the sand behind him. He turned sharply, spotting a black wolf stalking up to him, with blood still fresh on its tongue. A little behind, he saw the rest of the pack, moving in just as slowly. They came back for a feast, but they weren't expecting this second course.

Nox raised his pistol. This time, he felt no reluctance to kill.

Chapter Five

ONE MAN, FIVE WOLVES

Nox turned slowly, flicking back his coat on the left side to reveal his second pistol. Oh, he knew he'd need that one too. He flexed his fingers, and the wolves flexed their fangs.

The first wolf leaped at him, snarling. It came with such force and ferocity that Nox barely had time to fire. The wolf didn't so much as die as eat those bullets, and choke and gargle on them. Nox side-stepped out of the way of its falling body.

Then the next came, fast and just as ferocious. It was smaller than the first, pressing itself against the ground before pouncing on him. He had to use his left arm to block its snapping mouth from taking his head clean off. He nestled his right pistol on his arm, pressing it between the beast's eyes. They say you couldn't tame nature, and in some respects you couldn't—but it didn't matter how wild you were. Bullets made you tame.

As the body of their companion fell limp, the next two wolves stalked in slowly. It looked like one of them wasn't sure if it should attack or run. It was a pity of sorts that word of the Coilhunter didn't spread in animal tongues too. Maybe then they'd know for sure that they should've ran.

But there was a fifth wolf, and he saw it circling around him on the right. It was farther off, but as it circled, it came in a little closer. Those other two weren't just cautious. They were a distraction. Nox turned suddenly to the predator, keeping one pistol on the other two. It froze. Maybe it wasn't used to this. Maybe it was used to catching its prey off guard.

Nox could've filled them all with lead, but he was hoping to scare them off. He had a feeling in his gut he'd need all the ammunition he could find, so he certainly didn't feel like wasting any. It wasn't like he had access to his supplies in his trusty monowheel, or those in his hideout in the Canyon Crescent. He wasn't just lost. He was low. So, he had to make everything count. Right now he counted three bullets spent. He wasn't sure how long it'd be before he'd have to spend blood.

The dominant wolf on his right didn't budge. That was good, of course, but it didn't just mean it wasn't attacking—it wasn't running either. It sniffed the air, and a curious look formed in its eyes. Some of the ferocity faded from it, but Nox knew not to be fooled by that. He had the scars of many animals that feigned meekness just before the kill.

Then it dawned on Nox that it might've caught the scent of its kin on him. It'd been about a week since he stumbled upon Umna in the north-western stretches of the Wild North. She was a tribal woman, a guide for folk like him, and she had a tamed wolf by her side. It remembered him and nudged its head against his legs. Not quite a pet, and not quite wild.

Umna said she preferred it like that.

So, it left its scent. And this wolf, this larger, hungrier, *wilder* wolf, tried to reconcile the smell of man and the wild. Funny, that. This unmarked place was causing confusion for all.

It was then, as they gunned each other down with their glares, that Nox noticed they were wearing collars too. The fur obscured them, but they were there. And they looked just like the one he wore. He wasn't sure what to make of it. Not quite a slave, and not quite wild.

Throughout all this, Old Reliable moaned and whinnied fearfully. Nox couldn't calm him, not while he was killing the calm with his iron clap of thunder, not while the living wolves were snarling, and the dying ones were gargling in their death throes. The only calm was in the Coilhunter's unwavering, unshaking hands, in the untrembling twitch of his fingers. He could've gunned them all down, could've made it thunder even more. Then, only then, would the true calm follow in the wake of the storm.

But something else happened that the Coilhunter did not expect. Out of the corner of his eye, he saw one of the unmoving wolves start to spasm. Oh, the dead spasmed. They made a living show of it sometimes, as if Death were an unskilled puppet master. But this was different.

Nox stepped back slowly, slow enough to lower one hand towards his belt, where instinct told him he'd need to pull out something better than a pistol. Slow enough to watch the three living wolves back off. Slow enough to see the two dead ones come back to life.

Chapter Six

BELIEVER

The Wild North was the frontiers, but that didn't just mean of civilisation. It was the edge of everything. It was a place that seemed to straddle worlds. It didn't matter if you came doubting. It didn't matter if you questioned all and answered less. No matter what your personal convictions, the Wild North'd make a believer out of you.

Nox stepped back, almost stumbling over Old Reliable behind him. He'd seen many things—monstrous things—but so far he hadn't seen the dead rise, though he'd heard tell of it before. Why, he'd rationalised it all, like he always did. Maybe they weren't quite dead. Maybe it was the tug of ligaments, the spasm of muscle. Or maybe, just maybe, they were what the crazy called them—deadwalkers.

As he tried to collect his thoughts, and didn't feel he was collecting them quick enough, his instincts took over. And he was lucky they did. The first raised wolf snapped at his leg, but he moved out of the way of its jaws just in time. It still had the bullet nestled between its eyes, those glazed-over eyes, which should've been staring up at the sky instead of him.

The second wolf turned and jumped, almost

before it even looked where it was jumping. It was working on instinct too. Nox tumbled outs of its path, launching himself right over Old Reliable's body. The horse tried to buck and kick, but there was no energy for bucking, and no legs for kicking. If Nox were a heartless man, as some liked to paint him, he could've used the horse's body for cover. It was a funny thing. He'd rather use the bodies of men.

So Nox did what instinct told him. He cupped a few butterfly capsules from his belt and scattered them into the sand before the wolves. They leaped away as the little orbs rolled to their feet, or snapped at them, or howled at them. Then the capsules burst open, and out came dozens of small, mechanical butterflies, all hungry for movement, and all with a bellyful of sleep-inducing gas.

Nox stayed still, with his gloved hands on Old Reliable's head, trying to calm him. The wolves, however, roamed, thinking this an easy prey. They'd seen insects before. They'd swatted them away, or devoured them whole. These colourful kin were no different. And yet, they were.

The first snarling, leaping wolf, with its glazed eyes and blood-covered brow, took a lungful of the noxious gas, and slumped to the ground. The second increased its pace, but this only drew the butterflies to it all the faster. They flitted around, grasping onto its face with their tiny hook-like claws. It tried to shake them, but the shaking only lured more of them in. It howled through the haze, then coughed, then fell.

The other three wolves fled in terror. That they fled from other apparent creatures of nature was of little consequence to them. The Wild North was for the wild. You lived in the wild and died *to* the wild. Maybe it'd be another wolf, or maybe, in this crazy world of Altadas, it'd be a butterfly.

Those little insects finished with the wolves and came now for Old Reliable, who Nox couldn't calm enough to keep still. They sprayed their gas into the sorrel's face, sending him to sleep. That was a better sleep than the one Nox had planned for him, but only if he had good dreams. Nox almost never did.

"Dream deeply," he said. *Deeply*, because you didn't want to dream too close to the surface, when the surface was all sand and sun.

The butterflies flitted around him. He didn't swat them away, and he didn't sleep. His mask filtered out their gas, just like it filtered out the unclear air, just like it protected his tender lungs from the growing industry of the Iron Empire and the war down south. He could feel the oxygen tank on his back, pumping in that precious gas, along with a concoction of other chemicals to help reduce the swelling, to help numb the pain. They were the inspiration for the butterflies. Sometimes he just wanted to put the world to sleep, to take away the pain. That he did it with flair and colour was an homage to his days as a toymaker, back when this all started, back when he was Nathaniel Osley Xander, and not the Man with a Thousand Names.

He tapped a button on the wristpad attached to his left arm. The butterflies stopped flapping and dropped suddenly all around him. It was almost symbolic. You could sleep all you liked, and you could make the world around you seem colourful, but sooner or later it'd all come tumbling down. Then all you'd see is the desert, that constant killer called "the land." In a way, it was kind of soul-destroying, but if you had enough determination, you could find it inspiring.

So that's what Nox did. He scooped together his little toy butterflies, holding one up to the light to inspect the tiny glass cylinder, now empty. He loaded them back into his belt and replaced them with his favourite toys: his guns. See, Nox was a killer too, though he only killed the worst of what the wild had to offer. And it offered a lot.

He strolled over to the two sleeping wolves. It was hard to make out exactly what they were. Were they already dead? Could the dead even sleep? No doubt he could've held a sermon here, and he would've gotten a following. That was a how a lot of those cults started, by someone stumbling onto a miracle, and making others think they were the one behind it.

No, Nox thought, thinking now of the Man with the Silver Mane. *It's you. You're behind this.*

He pointed each pistol at the wolves, and fired. He now knew why his gut told him to save those bullets. He didn't think he'd have to kill the same wolf twice. He only hoped that the phrase *third time's the charm* wasn't quite what charmed these beasts.

Chapter Seven

NOT A LEG TO STAND ON

Now, Nox wasn't just lost. He'd come to terms with that, sure enough. Now he had to come to terms with everything else, with seeing the dead rise, and putting them down again. By rights, out here, wherever here was, he hadn't a leg to stand on—but he kept on standing, and kept on walking. That was something the land thought him. That was something the sun thought him. You persevered, maybe only out of spite, but you did it anyway. You eyed the sun and said: *You ain't lightning my funeral pyre.* You scooped up a handful of sand and said: *You ain't burying me yet.*

Then Nox thought of his former captor. *You ain't getting away with this.*

He left Old Reliable sleeping. He hadn't the heart to end him, and thought maybe he'd fade off in his dreams. That was the best way to go, so long as you didn't go in the middle of a nightmare. In many ways, that's how most did, but they were waking ones. Often times, they were the Coilhunter.

He ventured on, looking for the trail of those fleeing wolves, but the wind covered it quick, or he was lost again. Either was equally likely and unlikely, and altogether unhelpful. He kept trying to mark terrain features on the map of his mind, but the land here had a way of looking different every time you glanced at it, just like the eyes of the Man with the Silver Mane. He tried to breadcrumb his way, but the sand was even hungrier than he was. As much as he wandered by foot, he also wandered in his mind, drifting from thought to thought, from a glimpse at some future bounty to a half-forgotten memory.

He remembered hearing of the Resistance's attack on the city of Blackout in the south, and how the Regime had sent the Iron Guard to take it back. Those were the Iron Emperor's personal guard, and they were formidable. You see, they were half-man, and half-machine, and both halves made an abomination. Taberah Cotten, the so-called "Scorpion" of the Resistance, sent one of their bodies up to Nox for inspection. He still had it in his workshop, strapped and chained in case either part of it woke up. General Rommond had put an iron-piercing bullet in it, and by rights that meant it was dead, both the human and mechanical parts. But there wasn't much right in the Wild North, and Nox was starting to get used to surprises.

He heard something. A whisper. He looked around, expecting to see something else he'd dismissed as the rumours of children. There was nothing there. And yet, he felt like there was. There was a widespread belief among the tribes that machines had their own spirits, that they could communicate the secrets of mechanics in ways that nothing else could. There was one man who folk said was a living testament to that, a man more skilled than Nox with machinery, but all he was now was a testament to the dead. Brooklyn, they called him, though he had another name among the tribes. The Coilhunter had wanted to meet him, to learn from him, but the war got him before he ever got the chance.

Nox was no tribesman. As much as the desert tried to pry his eyes open to things beyond his reasoning, he wasn't one for dancing around campfires and singing for rain. There'd been a lot of dancing and singing over the years, and a lot of campfires, but there hadn't been much rain. Yet as much as the Coilhunter had his doubts about spirits and magic, he'd seen enough to know that he couldn't yet explain everything in this world. Well, he was no philosopher either. He was content to explain enough with his gun.

He tried to focus back on the path, but the whispers increased, until they almost seemed to come from everywhere around him. There was a paradox in them, for they seemed both distant and near, and both inside and outside of him. That was one reason he wasn't keen on the spirit world. He liked the simplicity of Dead or Alive. The other reason hurt more deeply, and he though part of him desperately wanted to hear his family's voices, he tried just as desperately not to listen.

"Whaddya want?" he barked to the land around him. Of course, the land wanted him, wanted to chew him up and leave just his own spirit voice. But the land didn't answer. The spirits did.

"Adoo alla kanna," they said, though maybe it

was just the way the wind sighed, the way his boots creaked, the way his hair rustled. Everything had a voice, and maybe everything had a language. Or maybe it was all just gibberish and the Coilhunter'd finally cracked like folk said he would.

"What does that mean?" Nox asked.

"Adoo alla kanna," the voices repeated. The wind repeated. His boots repeated. His hair repeated.

Nox rolled his eyes and sighed. "One of those answers then." It was like saying the definition of a word was the word itself. You either knew it or you didn't. You couldn't teach it to someone. Well, Nox was used to teaching folk, and he only ever thought them one thing.

Adoo alla kanna, he mused. The voices seemed to hear his thoughts just as much as his spoken words. They knew he didn't understand, but they made no effort to enlighten him—at least, none that he could see. Maybe he'd need the vision powder or the journey tea if he was to figure this one out, but first he'd have to figure out where he was.

And then he stumbled into something. His boot struck something metal in the ground. He halted and got out some of his tools, digging around the object. It took him longer than he liked, but not long enough to realise it was part of his own old reliable, his monowheel. That vehicle'd got him out of many scrapes in the past, but it'd got him into this one. And it most certainly wasn't going to get him out. Not in this shape. Not in this many widely-dispersed pieces.

"Well, howdy," Nox said with a kind of affection bikers shared with their hogs. He patted the chassis like he did the horse's mane. "I ain't got a bullet for you," he said, thinking back to Rommond's iron-piercing rounds, a technology the Coilhunter had first created, and then shared for the war effort. He always considered himself outside of that war, but that didn't mean his weapons had to be.

He pulled the piece out of the sand and bunched up all the loose wires. It was junk, fit for the iron walls of the Rust Valley—or maybe Porridge's scrap collection—but it was his junk. He thought he might be able to salvage something.

"Adoo alla kanna," the voices spoke again, prodding deeper into his mind. He got the impression they'd directed him to this severed piece of machinery, and that his wandering thoughts about the Iron Guard weren't so wandering at all. Maybe they were *guided* thoughts.

Nox cradled the machinery like a child. It reminded him, a little painfully, of how he held little Ambrose when she was born. It reminded him, stabingly, of how he held her when she died. He thought, a little guiltily, of how he'd pondered Mrs. Mayfield's idea in the Rust Valley, of how he wondered if machines could bring them back to him.

He was so lost in thought that he hadn't realised he was walking again. He wasn't sure where he was going, and he only knew he was backtracking when he found Old Reliable again. That stubborn horse just wouldn't die. Maybe he was waiting for Chance Oakley. Well, he'd be waiting a long time. Longer than he had, stubborn or not.

"Adoo alla kanna," the voices urged, and they

were stubborn too.

"Ah, I'd do all, but cannot," Nox replied grumpily, as if those voices were just a taunting child or a nagging wife. How we wished for those taunts and nags right now.

Then he paused and looked at the hanging wires in his arms. They looked an awful lot like ones he'd yanked out of that Iron Guard solider back in his workshop. They looked an awful lot like the ones he'd studied in its limbs.

"Hmm," he said, and even that was full of grit.

He knelt down, placing the machinery next to Old Reliable. The horse raised his head and showed his teeth. He still had a lot of fight in him. He still had a lot of life in him. Nox was starting to slowly realise that maybe he'd get to see Oakley after all.

Nox took one of his knives out, and Old Reliable flinched. Something was telling him to connect one of the severed ligaments with a wire. That shouldn't have done anything, but the tribesfolk said the spirits of machines course through wires like blood through veins. Maybe it wasn't so much a merging of two things. Maybe it was just plain old possession.

The Coilhunter followed his gut. It usually told him when to sling a gun, when to dodge, when to cast a butterfly cannister. Now it wasn't listening for the flaws of his enemies. It was listening to some phantom voices. Or the voice of his imagination.

He carved up that remnant of his monowheel, fashioning it into a pair of metal legs. He ran the wires though them and made himself into a witch doctor for a day. They say old dogs don't learn new tricks, but Nox's fingers were dancing now. Or maybe he was just barking.

By the end of it, which came far quicker than it should've, that blonde sorrel had a new pair of legs. The test, and it was a big one, was if they weren't just to make him pretty. Nox helped the horse up onto his unsteady limbs. For a while, it just looked like he was resting on those metal stilts. Then he took a step forward, and the metal moved.

"Adoo alla kanna," Nox said to Old Reliable, who whinnied playfully.

That was when he heard a different voice, the voice of the tribeswoman Umna.

"We are all connected," she said, and he turned to see her, but she wasn't there.

Chapter Eight

CANINES AND CANYONS

O ld Reliable had a new set of stompers, but that didn't mean he had steady feet. He trembled and stumbled like a foal taking his first steps. Nox guided him as much as he'd been guided to this strange discovery. He wasn't quite sure if he'd made an abomination himself, or an abomination *of* himself, but what he did know was that he'd need Old Reliable to help him find his way home.

Nox had a hurried lunch with a can of beans, exposing the scarred skin around his mouth to the sun, which'd be happy to do a little more scarring. He didn't have to hide his appearance from Old Reliable, who didn't judge him, and might've been a little self-conscious of his own. They were two of a kind now, the scarred and the ugly. Nox gave the horse some sunflower seeds from one of his pouches, but the sorrel was more focused on getting used to his new legs than anything else.

And it was just as well, because he'd need them soon enough.

Nox started when he heard a far-off howl. He cast the bean can in the direction of the sound, as if it were just another one of his gadgets. Oh, he'd made some like that before, especially early on. Folk said beans could be explosive, and they really were when Nox bundled dynamite into the can. But right now, it was just good old-fashioned tin and a worn-off label. The Coilhunter knew he'd have to save his gadgets.

He raced to Old Reliable, who was looking frantically back and forth for the direction of the howl. He was still unsteady on his feet, but he got a lot steadier in the moment. Fear had a way of doing that. Panic had a way of doing it fast.

"I'd have given you more time," Nox said, "but they're not givin' us any."

He climbed on slowly, out of courtesy for the horse's new limbs, even though he wanted to hop on fast. Old Reliable's legs almost buckled, just like Nox's did when he first awoke in the Lostlands. The Coilhunter hopped down, now painfully aware that he hadn't fully shaken off his own aches. He spun the barrel of his revolver, eyeing the bullets solemnly. He grew more solemn when he heard a chorus of howls following the first. He hadn't enough for the choir.

The wolves appeared on the horizon, gathering in a formidable line of silhouettes. There, against the backdrop of the sun, they looked a little more deathly, even if most, or all, of them were still living their first life. There was something about them that wasn't right. Nox could almost see it from here: the glint of sunlight off their iron collars.

Are you huntin' me? he asked the Man with the Silver Mane. *'Cause I'm huntin' you.*

The wall of darkness advanced, dropping down a dune like a black waterfall. Nox looked into Old

Reliable's eyes and pleaded with his own. He knew he couldn't outrun the tide on foot. He wasn't even sure about doing it on horseback. But maybe, just maybe, those iron legs'd help.

Old Reliable was aptly named, because he bowed his head towards the Coilhunter, nudging him to get on. The horse could still smell the scent of Chance Oakley on Nox. Maybe he thought that the Coilhunter was his breadcrumb back to him. Or maybe he just wanted to run from the wolves.

Well, he ran.

Old Reliable ramped up from trot to canter to gallop in just a dozen or so strides. There was something in those iron legs alright. Maybe there were spirits there after all.

The wolves came after them swiftly and frenzied. They kicked up the sand as they went, until the dust danced like devils between them. Their eyes were red and manic. Their maws were wide and gaping, just waiting to swallow their prey, rider and all.

Nox rode on, faster, urging Old Reliable on with his own, not-quite-iron legs. He didn't whip or lash, and he was never a man to wear spurs—but then his typical iron steeds never needed them. All he needed was a connection with the animal, and the unified fear of what came hounding behind them.

They almost tumbled down one dune, then struggled up another. They were momentarily calmed by an open expanse, until the expanse showed the dozen demonic hounds behind them. They raced south—until the south began to drop away.

They came suddenly through a sandy haze to

find the land cracked in great chasms, where the yellow and red sands fell down into shadowy abysses. The gaps varied, some just millimetres apart, others the size of a hand, and others still several feet across. They wormed through the earth, thinner here and fatter there, like monsters of nothingness. They were perfect for the Lostlands.

Chapter Nine

THE MONSTERS OF
NOTHINGNESS

It was too late to halt, and far too late to turn back. The tide had come in, and it was black. Nox drove Old Reliable like that sorrel was a monowheel. He yanked the reins like levers. He shifted his weight like he did inside the frame of his old vehicle. He made that horse turn and tilt as the land gave way around it.

They leaped, and the jump seemed like forever. Nox felt himself rise out of the saddle, and he clutched the reins all the tighter. Old Reliable came down hard on the other side of the first, two-foot ravine. He almost skidded, but Nox leaned him into the skid, drove those stumbling legs into another gallop. They'd cleared the first hurdle, but the course before them had many more. The race would be tight. The winners'd get to keep their lives.

They jumped again, this time over a smaller gap, which was followed by a series of tiny cracks the horse could ride across freely. If Nox'd had his monowheel, those thick landship treads might've bridged the distance, and if they didn't, he had spring-loaded grapnel hooks to get to the other side. But he didn't have his monowheel. He had a living, breathing creature, who tired and hungered, who feared and faltered, and who didn't run on diesel.

Well, run on fear, boy, Nox urged. Now, *there* was a lash that worked.

He rode Old Reliable not just over the varying gaps, but left and right as they narrowed and opened to varying degrees. This wasn't just to find the shortest holes to jump, but to confuse and split the wolves, and hopefully see one or two of them tumble down below.

But these wolves had that odd look in their eyes, like they were not altogether wild, but a caged wild. A wild that moves at the lash of another. Nox could see the Man with the Silver Mane in their stare.

The wolves howled, and their howls seemed to encourage the slower of them to pick up speed, and the quicker of them to become a little faster. It was their battle cry. All Nox had for a battle cry now was gunpowder, and he didn't want to waste that on warning shots. They'd already gotten a warning. The problem was: death wasn't warning enough.

"Go, boy," Nox said, as Old Reliable baulked at an eighteen-foot drop ahead of them. He was no Ootana horse, so he didn't scare easy, but you didn't need to scare easy to not want to risk a jump like that. Yet, when death is hot as hell on your heels, you either toss the coin in hopes of life ahead, or you turn around and sign that guarantee.

Nox's voice gathered up enough grit to be grim. "Go."

That horse's name wasn't just a title—it was a mission. He must've known he'd have to almost step off the edge before making the jump, in case he leaped too early, and leaped into an early grave. He damn well just rode off into the ravine, launching himself across at the final second, just barely making it to the other side.

Old Reliable skidded to a halt, turning sharply. That gave Nox time enough to see one wolf attempting the jump. It failed, and fell. The howl seemed to go on forever into the blackness below. The other wolves sulked and scowled, pacing to and fro on the other side.

Nox almost smiled beneath his mask, and Old Reliable had no mask to hide his toothy grin. They took this moment to catch their long-held breaths. For now, the land had saved them.

Nox should've known the land would never do that.

Chapter Ten

THE LAND

The land quaked suddenly. The fissures widened in places and shrank in others. It was no longer good enough to zig-zag through the obstacle course, because now the course was changing. Now, this was more like the land Nox knew.

He dragged hard on the reins, pulling Old Reliable back from the brink of a new-found fissure. The horse halted fast, then rode lengthways across the new opening until they came to a narrower gap. He jumped, and even as he jumped, the gap opened beneath him, like the maw of the earth eager for a bite. They made it to the other side, and the land closed again behind them, in time for the wolves to follow with ease.

Yes, this was the land Nox knew. For now, it was the ally of the wolves.

Nox rode on, harder now, pushing those iron limbs to their limit. They pocked the earth like bullet holes. Maybe that was why the earth fought back.

Then suddenly the ground gave way beneath Old Reliable's hind legs. The horse slipped and his hind fell into a small crevice. He tried to climb up, but the more he scrambled, the more the earth crumbled away nearby. Nox leaped off and pulled on the reins, helping Old Reliable back onto more solid land. As Nox climbed on again, he knew not to gloat at snatching back the food from the earth. The land had many mouths.

They rode on, traversing gaps that grew and shrank at a moment's notice. Nox started to get a feel for them, the same kind of instinct that told him when to draw a gun. He communicated this gut feeling to Old Reliable with a thug of the reins, leading him right, now left, urging him on, and holding him back. It all played out in a matter of seconds, just like death did for most. You learned to act on your gut, and act quick, or you often never got to act at all.

Ahead, Nox spotted a field of bodies, long rotten, yet not long revealed by the sand. There were dozens of them, possibly from some old battle, or maybe bundled together over time like the tumbleweed of the dead. Maybe they were an omen, a sign pointing to go back, but there was nowhere to go back to. The Lostlands might as well've not had directions at all.

The land continued to shift, cracking here, sealing cracks there. A skeleton arm dangled down into a ravine, and the body followed swiftly after as the land crumbled away beneath it. Maybe it thought: *Finally, a grave.*

They rode on, trampling the bones. The torn clothes and crumpled hats became more torn and crumpled beneath the horse's feet. Maybe it was desecration. All Nox knew was that it was survival. He promised not to add another body to the pile. The best promises weren't the ones you said, but the ones you walked and hobbled and ran. At least then you got closer to fulfilling them.

Even as he tried to focus on the path ahead, his gunslinger eyes spotted the fallen guns near their fallen masters. The men had spent their blood, but they hadn't spent all their bullets. He wrapped the reins tight around his right wrist. Then he leaned left, until he shifted out of the saddle and hung parallel to the ground. It must've been quite a sight, like he was riding the horse sideways, and yet in the topsy-turvy world he'd found himself in, nothing was quite out of the ordinary. He held out his left arm, letting the fingers graze the sand. Old Reliable charged on, right through the bodies and the guns. Nox scooped up a break action rifle as he neared it, then yanked himself back up into the saddle. He thumbed the lever to let the barrel of the rifle tilt open, saw there was still a round inside, and then flicked it closed again.

A wolf raced along beside them, pulling closer, biting at the air nearby. It should've been careful, because the wind knew how to bite back. Nox rested the barrel on one arm, aimed, and then took that pup out of the race. Yet, another came up fast, and Nox knew there wasn't another round to fire in the single-shot rifle. So he fired the rifle itself. He swung it hard and heavy, right at the approaching wolf, which was almost smiling with glee at coming so close. The gun struck it in the jaw, and it yelped and stumbled away.

Nox scoured the landscape for another firearm. He scooped up a shotgun, but a wolf launched itself at him as he did. It caught the barrel in its teeth and almost yanked Nox off the horse altogether. So the

Coilhunter let it have that gun. He promised it'd have another one soon enough. Well, it came pretty soon in the form of a revolver, nestled lightly in its holster, just ripe for the picking. Nox didn't even check for ammunition. Firing was another way of checking. The wolf that was still carrying the shotgun in its jaws rolled into a dead heap, and another skidded into a pile of bodies as Nox fired the remaining round. Then it clicked empty, but Nox had a whole field of guns to choose from. There was a long-dead criminal called Nine-finger Nancy who would've given another finger for an arsenal like this.

But the field was fading. The bodies were growing thinner on the ground. That was saying something, as there must've been a hundred of them there in total. Nox could've pushed Old Reliable to keep running, but he could feel the sorrel slowing down. No, now was the time to stand their ground and fight. Well, he'd do it like a good old-fashioned wagon train, fighting in a circle. And he'd make that circle on the field of bodies.

He turned sharply, sharper maybe than those wolves expected, because a few of them skidded to a halt. He picked up guns, firing some of them before he'd even hoisted himself back up into the saddle. The wolves fell, and some of them got up and fell again. Nox knew there'd be more ammunition. Men usually killed each other before they clicked dead. You see, you didn't just have a bullet with your name on it. You had a lot of bullets spelling those letters out.

The land continued to crack, taking a body here and there, though not before Nox'd taken their guns. The earth might've thought it was fast—if it could think, and a lot of tribes said it could—but it didn't have the swiftness of a gunslinger. It didn't have the resourcefulness of a tinker. It didn't have the determination of a bounty hunter. Nox led Old Reliable through the maze of cracks and crevices, all the while whittling down the numbers of the wolves.

By the end of it, there were far fewer human bodies, and far more bodies of wolves. Nox had a single round left in his newly-plucked rifle, and there was one more coyote to kill. It circled them just as much as they circled the battlefield. This was a smart one. A careful one. A killing one. This was one that Nox knew wouldn't die just once. He could see the shimmer of lights on its collar, illuminating some strange symbols. Nox still had bullets in his own guns, but he'd promised to save them for the Man with the Silver Mane. He could see in the wolf's eyes that that man wanted to make him break his promise.

But the wolf wasn't the only clever animal. Old Reliable lured the wolf close to an emerging crack, then reared and bashed it with his iron legs. The wolf stumbled back, then slipped into the growing chasm. It didn't matter how many lives it had. It could live them all out in the dark below.

The land suddenly quietened, and the quakes faded into a dim earthen thunder. Old Reliable halted, and both he and his rider panted heavily. Nox watched for more wolves, but no more came. The land no longer shook. The earth no longer crumbled. Everything was peaceful now, but the Coilhunter couldn't help but wonder how long that would last.

Past lessons told him: not long enough.

Chapter Eleven

THE SHIFTING GRAVEYARD

They rested for a moment, but Nox wasn't keen on resting at a place where the earth breaks. It'd be evil luck to survive the battle only to fall into a ravine during the twists and turns of sleep. But then Nox left luck to the gamblers. When he went out to kill, he made sure he had all six rounds in his revolver.

The day was wearing on, and with it came a dust cloud that made it harder to rest and even more reckless to rest in the field of bodies. Nox led Old Reliable on by foot, making for what he thought was south. The needle of his compass acted erratically in the Lostlands, landing at random directions.

Nox paused when he heard a clunk. His foot hit the edge of something hard, something stone. Then, as the wind died down and the sand settled, he saw it.

A graveyard.

The tombstones went on for what seemed liked miles, though much of that was the mirage of the dead. They tilted here and there, and some were flat. But this was no ordinary burial ground. It was the Shifting Graveyard, a site that was once settled, but now seemed to roam across the vastness of the Wild North on the rolling dunes and whirling sands.

Some said it followed you. Some said it travelled ahead of you, marking out your trail of life with the edge of a tombstone. The names were worn down to nothing by the castigating winds, those same winds that rebuked the living and the dead. Some said the names had worn off for a reason—so the desert could carve yours there instead.

Amidst the mausoleum was a man, hunched over and resting his hands on a shovel. He was dishevelled, with long hair, some black and some grey, and of all varying lengths, as if some of it had been eaten by the wind. His face was craggy, and his nose was bent. All of his features looked like they were trying to collapse in on themselves. His back hunched. His arms hunched. His nose hunched.

Nox got back into the saddle, happy for the higher ground, and happier for the chance to ride away quick. Something about this gravedigger was off. Maybe it was because there really shouldn't have been a grave here. Nox slipped his pistol out quietly. As far as he was concerned, that shovel wasn't just for digging—it was a weapon.

"What is this place?" Nox asked. He'd heard tales of it before, but truth and tales mixed in the Wild North like there was no difference. Often, there wasn't. Sometimes you doubted the truth and believed the lies. Well, the land'd fix that for you. It'd make a lesson out of you.

"This is the Shifting Graveyard," the gravedigger said. "It is where the sand has taken the lost. Anyone who stumbles in the desert finds themselves here, sooner or later. Have you stumbled, Coilhunter?"

Nox cocked an eyebrow. "Have you?"

"I am the Keeper of the Shifting Graveyard."

"Leader of the lost," Nox mused.

"No," the man said. "Not me."

Nox almost growled. "*Him* then. The Man with the Silver Mane."

The old man's smile became a crescent moon, and it was crooked too. If there was magic in him, it was a slimy, snakey magic, the kind that tricksters and conmen gravitated to. It was the kind of magic that deserved a Wanted poster. But Nox wasn't here for a gravedigger. He was here to dig fresh graves.

"Are you one of his lackeys?" Nox rasped.

The old man grinned. "We all are." He ran his index finger between his collar and throat.

Nox stared at him coldly, keeping his gun pointed, letting the iron stare even colder. "I'm not," he said, letting the grit gather and add to his conviction. He said it like he said the first words of the hunt and the last words before the kill. It wasn't just a promise. To him, it was law.

"So you say," the old man croaked. "So you think."

"So I am."

"For now."

"Forever."

The gravedigger's eyes were wry. "He'll win you over."

"Will he, now?"

"He'll work his magic on you."

Nox spun the barrel of his revolver. "Maybe I'll work mine on him."

"Do you even know what he *is*?" the old man

53

asked.

"A man."

"More than a man."

"Well, I've killed folk who thought they were more than men. They died like men all the same."

The old man eyed him with a twinkle. "They'll come back to haunt you, Coilhunter."

"Well, I guess I'll have to start hunting phantoms then. It wouldn't be the first time I've chased ghosts."

"You won't kill him," the man continued, consulting the lines in his hands for answers. "You'll just release him."

"Will I, now?"

"It is so."

"And what about you? What'll you do?"

"I'll serve my master, in life and in death." He paused and ran a long, bony finger under his nose. "Especially in death."

"Your master," Nox said. "Where can I find 'im?"

"You can only find him if he wishes to be found."

"That's not what I asked."

"But that's what I answered."

"Well, you better change your answer, or I'll change you from gravedigger to gravesleeper."

"The Lost Tribe," the man said in time.

"Who're they?"

"More who serve."

"Well, ain't that a surprise."

"They camp not far from here, due west."

"If only I knew where *here* was," Nox grumbled.

"You do. This is the Lostlands."

Nox forced a smile. "Aptly named."

"So are the Lost Tribe."

"They won't stay lost for long," Nox promised. "And if they're in league with the Man with the Silver Mane, they probably won't stay alive for long either."

The gravedigger's eyes widened with a kind of glee at the thought. "I better get digging then," he said. For a moment then, his shovel looked less like a shovel and more like a staff.

Nox'd heard much about the so-called Magi, who claimed to have come from the land of Iraldas across the sea, a world with different races and different rules. In Altadas, they'd been roped into the war effort by the Resistance, tasked with making contraceptive amulets to keep women protected from having so-called "demon" children. Yet every now and then a Magus worked alone, serving only himself. Nox didn't know what to make of those fables. For a long time, he thought they were only designed to give hope to the losing faction in the war. Now, he wasn't so sure.

Nox rode away, then paused and looked back. "What do I call you, gravedigger?"

The man looked up and contorted his face in thought. "Perhaps ... the Last Man you See?"

"No," Nox said. "That's me. If you're bad."

"And am I bad?"

Nox eyed him up and down. "We'll find out, sooner or later. Sure as the sand."

As Nox rode off, the gravedigger called after him. "No. Sure as the grave."

Chapter Twelve

THE LOST TRIBE

Nox followed the gravedigger's directions, which weren't much to go on. He was starting to doubt himself, and had long started to doubt the gravedigger, when one of Old Reliable's iron feet unearthed a black feather. Not the feather of a tamba bird, the now-mythical creature that was used by some tribes to symbolise peace—and which unsurprisingly went extinct with the arrival of the Iron Empire. No, not even the feather of a raven, or a vulture, or some other beast of the air. This was a man-made feather. And whenever you found man-made things, you found men multiplying nearby.

For now, all Nox found was feathers.

He strolled on, slower now, the kind of slow he'd do when entering a saloon full or criminals or a town full of scum. The desert still looked mighty empty, except for those few black feathers, but it somehow felt he'd arrived someplace. It was no surprise that here, in the Lostlands, it wasn't signposted.

"Howdy, my feathered friends," Nox rasped. He parked Old Reliable and glanced around. There was no one within eyeshot, though there was the feeling of many. The Coilhunter's hand got another feeling into it: that familiar, long-trained itch.

"Now, boys," Nox said. "Let's see some faces."

"Or what?" a voice, deep and muffled, said from just feet ahead.

"No, that's a voice," Nox said. "Now, show me a face."

Suddenly, the sand erupted, and out of a hole in the ground came a man cowled in feathers. His entire face was covered by a black mask with a raven's beak, all except the eyes, which stared out at Nox with a kind of tranquillity the Coilhunter rarely saw in men.

"Still not a face," Nox said, "but that'll do."

"Why you do not show yours?" another tribal voice said, and another man, similarly attired, rose from the sand on the right. Two more followed on the left.

Nox barely budged on the saddle. But boy did his fingers itch.

"I'll take it you're the Lost Tribe," Nox said.

"We are," the first man replied. He was taller than the rest, mostly due to a higher cowl and larger plume of feathers. Their masks muffled their voices just like Nox's did, but theirs didn't breathe out black smoke. Nox let out a timely puff.

"What's with the get-up?" the Coilhunter asked. He gestured to their outfits with his left-hand pistol. They hadn't noticed him taking it out. He wanted to draw their attention to it now.

"What is with yours?"

"Survival," Nox said, though he knew it was about flair as well. An old friend called Porridge would've said it was all about the latter. He was of the mind that men peacocked around in cloth and leather, but Nox was of the mind that men peacocked with knives and guns.

"What do you want, Coilhunter?" The tribesman's accent was new to Nox, a mix of the tribes of the North and the walled-ones of the so-called Civilised South. Nox couldn't help but think it a strange mix.

"Directions."

"Just directions?"

"Well, somethin' tells me there ain't anything *just* about what you do, nor where I'm goin'," Nox said. "But for now, directions'll do fine."

"To where?"

"I call him the Man with the Silver Mane."

The tribesfolk looked at each other curiously. They weren't familiar with that title, clear enough, but you could see in their eyes that they were familiar with the man behind it.

"I'm bettin' you've got a similar name for 'im," Nox added.

"We have only our own names," the leader said. "No one can name another."

"Is that so?" Nox asked. He wondered where he'd gotten so many titles from then. It seemed like not a day went by without some other gang or conman giving him a new one. The Man with a Thousand Names was apt, but one day even that title might be an understatement.

"So, what'll I call you?" Nox said.

"Rassa-tuja-kissa," the man replied. There was something about how he said it that made it sound a little off. The voice was muffled, but it seemed like the accent changed a little. Nox was no expert on the tribes, but this kind of sounded like how someone would put on their voice to mock them. Like how the Southfolk might do it.

"Well, Rassa, what's the deal with your tribe?"

"There is no deal."

"What about the feathers?"

"You insult us to ask."

"Maybe I do, but call me curious."

"Curious is not your name."

"You've got that right, Rassa. Call me Nox."

"That is not your name either," Rassa said. "*Nathaniel*," he hissed.

"Don't make me draw on you."

"Do not think we did not already see you draw."

Nox smiled with his eyes. "No, you saw me draw one gun. Don't make me draw the other."

Then suddenly the tribesfolk shifted and drew weapons of their own. Except, they weren't guns. They pulled out long polearms from inside their robes. That would've been bad enough, except these ones pulsed with a little-known thing called electricity.

Chapter Thirteen

ELECTRIC

The tribesman to the right raised his polearm up high above his head, ready to bring it down on Nox and Old Reliable, but he ended up bringing it down on himself when Nox fired a bullet into his wrist. They say everyone's got a gun hand, but Nox'd proven that wrong by leaving some folk with no hands at all.

Nox fired with his other gun at the two tribesmen on the left, but they parried the blasts by spinning their polearms rapidly, until the whiz of electricity filled the air. Nox pulled on the reins and drove the horse back, then right.

Rassa swung his polearm low, and it struck the front legs of Old Reliable. The electricity bounced up those iron limbs and gave poor Old Reliable a jolt. The horse toppled, and Nox rolled off just in time to avoid being crushed beneath him.

Nox cast a butterfly capsule as he rolled. The mechanical butterflies inside barely had time to hatch before Rassa swooped in, tearing them apart with his rotating weapon. Any that survived were attracted by the buzz of electricity and the motion of the polearm, and they were electrocuted.

So much for nature, Nox thought, though it was his own breed of nature. He bred them by the bucket load in his hideout in the Canyon Crescent. Well, he didn't have buckets of them now to waste, so held on to the remaining capsules. He'd have to do this the old-fashioned way. It was lucky he was good at that too.

Nox pointed his pistol, half-clicked the trigger, then dropped it and quickly rose and fired the other. This put Rassa right off, sending him stumbling back, frantically fending off the bullets. Boy did he spin that polearm, and the bullets pinged off it like a shield. He heard a grunt nearby as a bullet bounced into another tribesman, sending him sprawling to the desert floor. Nox didn't intend to kill these folk, because he didn't entirely know if they were bad, or just slaves of bad. But as far as Nox was concerned, this one was on Rassa.

The next two were on Nox, and boy did they swoop in quick. They came together, like a team. One polearm came down vertical, while the other swung horizontal, hoping to catch him whichever way he went. Nox dodged and ducked, kicking the legs out from under one of them. He tried to brace himself with the polearm, but Nox kicked that out too, sending it spinning between Nox and the remaining tribesman. It was a good distraction, good enough for Nox to send him limping from another bullet. Some said Nox shot gun hands. Well, he did feet too. And boy were you lucky if that's all he did.

Rassa came in fast, but Nox parried the blow with the fallen polearm. The electricity sparked between them. It highlighted the grimness of the Coilhunter's eyes. They pressed against each other harder like the locked antlers of fighting deer. They puffed their chests. They challenged each other in the moment, urging the other to take a half-step back, to let their arm slip a little.

"These are some weapons you've got here," Nox said.

Rassa didn't reply. He was struggling against the Coilhunter's larger frame, but he wasn't giving in any time quick. Both of them pushed the electricity closer to the other, waiting for the moment when the other fried. Nox wasn't entirely sure how bad it'd burn, but he had his own small supply of electricity back at his workshop to know that it could give a nasty shock.

Rassa was just about to baulk. Nox could see it in his eyes. The tranquillity turned to strain, then came close to panic. Oh, he knew how bad it burned. He'd used these weapons before. Nox could almost see the kills in his eyes. What he could see for certain was that Rassa wasn't like the rest. No, he was no slave of bad. He was bad too.

Then, at the final moment, when Rassa was forced to take a step back to balance himself, Nox's hand slipped a little and struck a button on the polearm, turning the electricity off. Rassa's eyes changed to opportunity now, but Nox took it first. He quickly flicked the weapon, tapping off the button on Rassa's side, removing the voltage there as well. Then he swung and jabbed the end of the staff into Rassa's stomach, knocking the wind from him. He stumbled back into the dirt.

"Right," Nox said, marching up to Rassa and grabbing him by the neck. He yanked the cowl clean off, and Rassa was lucky he didn't take off the head. Nox was surprised to see the face beneath: a pale man with short, tight hair. Not the average tribesman at all.

"Well, now," Nox said. "Ain't that a sight for sore eyes."

Rassa scowled.

"Now, is that a tribesman's scowl," Nox said, "or is that the scowl of someone who just made up a tribe?"

"It is not made up," Rassa said, in his now too obviously fake accent. "We are real."

"Oh, you're real, alright. You just ain't what you say you are."

"We are Lost Tribe."

And boy, oh, boy were they lost. Some folk went to the tribes to find themselves, and some went out into the Lostlands when the tribes couldn't help them. Some weren't so much as looking for themselves as looking for a family, a community—a tribe. The Ootana were reluctant to welcome outsiders. The Rasaoua shunned them. The Udanudaga despised them. And the Tiandala were gone, all except Umna, wandering somewhere in the wild. Few spoke of the Anganda, and they were growing fewer for speaking of them.

"Well, I found ya," Nox said, and he said it like he did when he had a Wanted poster. Rassa wasn't on any that he knew, but he probably should've been. The Coilhunter knew it in his gut—his own old reliable— that if he looked hard enough, he'd find the remnants of Rassa's crimes. Why, he didn't think he'd have to look that hard at all.

Nox grabbed Rassa by the scruff of the neck and started hauling him away. Normally the body wouldn't have struggled. Normally the body wouldn't have fought back. He could've made it easier with a grasp, draw, and fire—three stages he'd long honed into what many saw as a single movement. He was getting older, but it felt like his gun hands were getting younger, getting quicker. Experience was their whetstone. Experience made him sharp and deadly. But no. The easier kill wouldn't be any use to him out here. He had to find a way to the Man with the Silver Mane. Rassa was the way.

Rassa did his best to shout out some tribal language he'd long been imitating. He didn't quite get it right, and it showed. Nox was no expert on the tribes of the Wild North, but he knew enough, and had met enough, to know what didn't look or sound right. Rassa was out of the ordinary, that's for sure. It made him right at home with the Man with the Silver Mane. *Ordinary* just didn't cut it with him.

"You can keep yammerin'," Nox rasped, "or you can save your voice for when I ask ya to speak." He leaned in close, blasting a puff of smoke out of his mask right into Rassa's face. "Because when I ask, you God damn better speak."

He didn't wait for Rassa's reply, and Rassa didn't give much of one beyond a few grunts. Nox dragged him on further, away from his supposed tribe. If the Coilhunter'd had his monowheel nearby, he would've hauled Rassa into the box at the back. The bounty box. Boy, you didn't want to find yourself there. It was small, and it wasn't particularly deep. But it was as good as a coffin. It was as good as a grave.

He halted and flicked a pouch open on his belt with his thumb. He rolled out a butterfly capsule, one of his favourite toys. It became part of the legend of him. He came in a cloud of dust, smoke, and gas. The gas came from the little mechanical butterflies—and they sent you off to slumber. It was just the ticket for someone like Rassa, whom Nox needed to subdue until he found a better wait to travel. And Nox could use it now. Rassa couldn't swat them away.

He held the capsule up to Rassa, who stared at it, frozen in fear. Why, it had that effect on many too. Sometimes the fear was greater than the weapon itself. It was as if he'd learned to bottle that too.

"Well," Nox said, "now's about time for bedtime prayers."

But Rassa didn't pray. Just as the Coilhunter was about to lay him down to sleep, the land decided to do the same for Nox. It broke apart beneath him, swift and sudden. He fell and let go of the capsule. Rassa snatched it from the air, before clambering away from the hole.

Nox landed on his feet, holding his hat over his eyes to shield them from the dust. When it cleared, he saw Rassa smiling down at him. It seemed he had a bounty box of his own.

Chapter Fourteen

PROSPECTOR

The thing about holes in the Wild North was that they usually didn't stay holes for long. The sand swept in and they filled up fast. Why, you didn't need a gravedigger for that. The whole damn desert was the gravedigger—and the grave. So if you found yourself in one of those holes, well, you'd better get out quick, or you might drown beneath the grains.

Nox'd already prepped the grapnel launcher on his right arm. He wasn't sure what it'd grasp onto. If it just took a handful of sand, it'd only help the land fill up the hole all the quicker. Some folk said you dug your own holes. Some others said you filled them up too, with you inside.

Except this one wasn't filling.

Nox paused, waiting to see a sandstream around the rim, like the trickle of an hourglass. Nothing. He watched where Rassa perched, waiting to see a heavier stream there. But nothing. Something was different about this hole. There was a reason why it hadn't filled up before.

Nox fired the grapnel up, but stepped out of the way immediately. He *knew* it would come back down. He just wanted to see it, to tick that little box in his head. And, sure enough, the hook bounced off what looked like an energy shield across the surface, and came back down disappointed. Nox flexed his wrist and it recoiled back into the launcher.

So, he thought. *You've got some kind of force field.* He'd heard theories about such technology, but they usually stayed theories. Both sides of the war down south were too busy funding things that'd kill you to worry too much about things that'd it stop you getting killed. There was certainty in good old iron. Force fields and the like were as good as magic— and magic wasn't much good in Altadas. The Magi had learned that when they came from Iraldas and found their spells wasted in the desert. Well, so they claimed. Some of them, or all of them, might've just been conmen spinning tales, like good old Sam Silver selling water machines. So the Regime and Resistance focused on the here and now, and they focused with guns and turrets. But here in the Wild North, away from the war, no one needed to worry about the short-term. They could play it long, and reach far. And maybe they'd pluck back something from beyond explanation, like their own kind of grapnel gun.

Rassa disappeared from view, and Nox resigned himself to not getting out by going up. They say when you're in a hole, you shouldn't keep digging, but the folk that said that weren't were Nox was. If anything, he *had* to dig. But they never said anything about where you stuck your shovel. Going down was one thing. Going sideways was something else. Nox'd already noted that the other tribesmen came from holes farther on. They must've been nearby. They must've led somewhere.

So he yanked the grapnel from the launcher, releasing a lever to slacken the cord. Then he bashed it against the rockface like a pickaxe. It reminded him of Chance Oakley, that one-time gold prospector. There was nothing much in gold now, of course. It was all in iron, ever since the Iron Empire, the so-called Regime, came into power. Even the Treasury cashed in for the new currency. There were a lot of folk who didn't agree with the Regime, but they still played by their rules. You called them the rich.

Nox hammered away, taking chunks out of the rock. Oh, the sand was filling up inside now. He was up to his knees in it. He was also painfully aware that the walls could cave in on him. Well, he was aware. He knew the pain would come later.

Then he struck something metal. To many prospectors, that sound was like the chink of coils. Maybe it was an iron vein. Maybe it was a future mine. Before you even found out for sure, you staked your claim to it. You started planning how you were going to defend it. Because they'd come. Oh, yes, they'd come. The looters. The robbers. The Regime. They'd all come with pickaxes of their own. And guns.

But Nox uncovered the metal before he made his judgement. It was iron alright, but it wasn't ore. It was a door. He forced it open, and it took some forcing. The walls shuddered around him. So he couldn't send the tribal leader to sleep. Well then, fair enough. Now it was time to wake the rest of the tribe.

Chapter Fifteen

CHASING RATS

The first of them spotted the Coilhunter almost instantly and ran. That was how most folk did it when they saw that mask or the buckled badge on his chest, with its five parts coloured to match those he hunted. And sometimes running got you places. More often than not, with the Coilhunter running after you, it got you places you didn't want to go. Like the Bounty Booth.

Nox didn't just have quick fingers. He had quick feet. He raced after the fleeting figure, turning corners sharply in the sandy maze. His shoulders grazed the walls, sending down the scree. His elbows took little chunks out. This wasn't just a maze. It was a cavern just waiting to cave in.

But the Coilhunter wouldn't make it wait.

Nox shoved his fist, and the grapnel launcher fired, punching a hole in the rock as the tribesman ducked and flitted around the corner. Nox ran right into the recoiling wire, hooking it back into place without a pause. It was like a self-loading gun. Except with this one you got to live.

He bolted after the tribesman, gaining speed by taking each turn harder, shouldering his way through the sand. By some accounts, this whole network of tunnels was its own kind of mines. Normally you didn't disturb the walls. But when the people who'd made the walls didn't have any qualms about disturbing you, then maybe you'd tear down the wallpaper like it was Wanted posters.

The tunnel shook and the sand came down heavy from the roof. No. Not the roof. The roof was held up with a force field here as well. It came down from the tops of the walls.

The figure halted, shielding his eyes. "You gamble!" he shouted at Nox. "The walls will cave in. You bet. You gamble!"

"No," Nox side, firing the grapnel hook into the wall behind the man. "I'm countin' on it." The hook grasped tight, and Nox yanked the wire, pulling down the wall on top of the tribesman.

Nox strode up to the figure, who was half-submerged in sand. The grapnel gave that familiar click as it latched back into place. He glanced up at the ceiling, where the sand still held behind the invisible force field.

"Now," Nox said. "You tell me how to get—"

"I never tell."

"Let me finish. You tell me how to get up there, or I'll tear down every wall tryin'."

"You are evil walled-one, attacking poor tribe."

"You ain't no tribe," Nox said. "Not a real one, anyhow. You're just as much a walled-one as I am. Except, now we're tearin' down those walls. I'm guessin' you ain't alone here. Maybe you've got a family." He found it hard not to let his chest heave at the thought. "Maybe you've got what you *call* a tribe. Maybe this is a home. Well, don't make me go wrecking the place if I don't have to."

"I never tell."

Nox sighed. He grasped a handful of sand and poured it over the tribesman's head. "Well then, let's just get this over with and let me bury you."

The tribesman spat and shook his head as the sand went into his eyes and mouth. Nox poured another handful, and then another, until the tribesman eventually called out, "Stop!"

Nox paused mid-trickle. "Well, come on now. The hourglass is tickin'."

"There is ramp up to world above in central chamber."

"And where's that?"

"Down there," the tribesman said, nodding to one tunnel. "Left, right, straight, two lefts."

"Well, I hope you ain't lyin'."

"We Dasawoota never lie."

Nox smiled with his eyes. "Yeah, and I thought you never tell."

The Coilhunter followed the directions, fending off attacks from a handful of other tribesmen, who came at him with basic weapons. He used a basic weapon of his own: a knife. But lucky for them, he didn't use the blade. The handle knocked them out just fine.

Nox turned the final corner, finding himself in a larger cavern with many tribesfolk standing in a circle around an electric-powered hearth. Behind them was an earthen ramp leading upwards. Daylight streamed in, stretching shadows.

"So, here you all are," Nox rasped. "The desert rats in their den."

He eyed them up and down coldly. They wore slightly different attire to the fighters up top, but it was still black and still feathers. They had different figures though. It seemed like they were the women.

It was then, as Nox glanced at the one on the far left, that he did a double-take. Beneath all those layers were a pair of luminous yellow high-heeled boots, which stood out even more against the black feathers above.

"Hmm," Nox said, cocking his head. "Well, howdy, Porridge."

Chapter Sixteen

DENFIGHTER

Porridge let out his familiar high-pitched yelp just as two of the other tribesfolk charged at Nox. They pulled out long staves, but these were just made of wood, and weren't electrified. That was arguably a good thing, but men had a habit of dying to just about anything. Wood'd do just fine.

"Oh!" Porridge cried. "Don't hurt him, peaches! Oh! Don't hurt *me!*" He frolicked around the room, hands in the air, simultaneously getting in and out of everyone's way.

Nox was even more reluctant to use his pistol here, not because they might be women, but because they might be innocent, just roped into the fight by the Man with the Silver Mane, who did a lot of roping. How he'd lassoed Porridge was God's guess. You'd think God would've known, but in the Wild North all God could do was wonder.

The staves came in hard, and Nox ducked the first, but took the second in the stomach. He hobbled back, grasping at the wall, which crumbled in his hands. He grunted through his pain and dove over another incoming staff, rolling on the ground on the other side. He caught the next one with both hands

73

and pushed the tribeswoman back. Oh, she was a woman alright, but she was big and broad, and she could hold her own. They tugged for a moment, back and forth, until Nox made a feint for his gun, then jabbed that staff back all the harder. Woman or man, they all fell the same.

Porridge pulled off his headdress, letting his golden-brown curls tumble out. He cast the hat away with dramatic flair, though he also threw it like it was something dirty, barely grasping it between two fingers. It somersaulted through the air, and at a glance it might've looked like a real crow. When it landed, it became a deathtrap for the nearest tribeswomen, who, in her haste to attack Nox, slipped on it and crashed to the ground.

Elsewhere, Nox continued to dash and dodge, sliding under swinging staves and jumping over others. He was tempted to throw out a butterfly canister, but he knew he'd have no way of getting back to his warehouse to make more. He had a feeling in his gut, where the gunslinger in him lived, that he'd need them for the Man with the Silver Mane. He had another feeling there that maybe they wouldn't be enough.

He grabbed a fallen staff and swung it wildly, warding off the other tribeswomen.

"Back off," he croaked. "I don't want to fight you."

A woman yelled as she came in fast, and he clubbed her senseless.

"I didn't say I *wouldn't* fight," Nox added.

The rest of them came in together. Nox parried their blows, yelping as he caught his fingers between his staff and one of theirs. He pushed one end up sharply, striking one tribeswoman on the chin, before ducking and sweeping low, tripping up another. Then one of them leaped on his back, clinging on to him with hands and feet. She grabbed one of the pipes leading from his mask to the oxygen tank on his back and tried to pull it loose. Nox stumbled backwards, bashing the woman against the rock behind him until she slipped off.

There were two women left, and one of them was about to charge when Porridge leaped on her back and clawed at her mask, shifting it around until the eyeholes were out of place. She stumbled around, in and out of the way of her comrade, who tried to move in on Nox, then on Porridge, and finally fell to the Coilhunter's grappling hook.

Porridge was still clutching the blinded tribeswoman, but he was the one who was screaming, not her. She turned around and around, and he hung on for dear life, until she toppled from the dizziness. Porridge rolled off, scrambled onto one elbow, then fainted with an "Oh!" Nox strolled over to the woman and stopped her vertigo by knocking her out with the end of the staff.

The room went suddenly silent, enough for Nox to hear his shifting boots. He gave the room another once-over before dropping the staff. It wasn't the first time he was the last man standing, even if these weren't all men. It wasn't a victory he was ever really proud of, because often he didn't really want to fight. But it was another day, so that meant another pile of bodies. These ones were just lucky that they still had beating hearts.

And there was one in particular Nox was interested in. He rolled Porridge onto his back and gently slapped the man's face. He was out cold, though his face was plenty warm. His cheeks were flushed, giving him a kind of jovial radiance, even when he was counting sheep.

"Nap time's over," Nox said. He yanked some smelling salts from his belt and almost stuffed them up the man's nose.

"Oh," Porridge said, coming round. "J-just a minute, plum. Just a minute." He rubbed his eyes and blinked rapidly before feigning surprise at seeing the Coilhunter. As usual, he feigned it with both hands in one more dramatic pose. "*You*, dearest!"

"Yeah, *me*," Nox grumbled. "But *I* should be the one who's surprised."

Porridge clung out of Nox as the Coilhunter got up, forcing Nox to help Porridge to his feet. That trader had a way of volunteering you to be his crane and anchor, lifting him up or keeping him in place. Porridge stumbled on the spot and clung on all the tighter.

"Oh!" Porridge cried. "My legs are like jelly. Jelly, sweetie. Jelly!"

"You're lucky you can stand at all."

"Oh, my spinning cogs! Don't remind me!" He placed the back of his hand against his forehead, as if he was about to faint again. "I'm not built for all this …," and he paused, biting his lip with a smile, "excitement."

"That's for sure," Nox said. "Great use *you* were."

Porridge pouted. "I did my part."

"Yeah, and you did it mostly lyin' down."

Porridge blushed and fanned his face. "Well, dear, I always do it best lying down."

Chapter Seventeen

PLUM

They followed the ramp up to the world above, and Nox had his guns at the ready. He half-expected Rassa to be there, waiting. But the other half was a wiser side. That half expected Rassa to be long gone. He was.

"Damn," Nox said. "Well, that was a waste."

"Oh, plum, I hope you don't mean rescuing me."

"No. Well." He gave a half-smile. It seemed he was doing everything in halves now. No wonder he couldn't catch his prey. "Depends how this whole thing turns out."

"Oh, don't make me a soothsayer!" Porridge cried. "My old dearest nanna, strawberry sweetheart though she was, used to say I'd be good at telling fortunes. Oh! I could faint at the notion."

"Well, don't."

"Oh, she had such dreams for me, little dandy that I was."

"Yeah, well, your dreams might be dead, but you ain't, so let's get walkin'."

They ventured out, following the faint trail of Rassa. He'd tried to hide his tracks, but he hadn't learned the true techniques of the tribes, so he wasn't that good at it. Nox could follow them with ease.

Porridge abandoned his feathers, revealing his usual attire. Well, that salvager didn't really have just *one* usual attire, but a whole selection. In fact, Nox wasn't sure he'd ever seen the man in the same clothes twice. Right now, he wore a frilled shirt that was half green and half purple, with little boxes of the opposite colour around the shoulders. Below that he wore black leather trousers, with a seam of yellow down the side. On his shoulders he wore a semi-translucent lace shawl, and around his neck he wore a rainbow-coloured scarf with periodic sequins.

"Oh, I feel so naked without a hat!" Porridge exclaimed, patting his curls delicately. "Oh, peach, imagine me naked. Oh!"

Just a few steps further on, Porridge stumbled in his heels.

"Oh!" Porridge cried, hanging out of Nox. "This'll be the death of me!"

"Why in God's name are you wearin' heels out here anyhow?"

"Oh, plum, God don't have no fashion." Porridge smiled. "It's up to the rest of us."

"Well, you should've picked something a little more practical."

"Oh, now don't you go pretending that you don't go for a little show every now and then, daisy. It's not all gunfire with you now, is it? No, dearie. Why, I know it's smoke as well."

"Let's just keep walkin'."

"Where are we walking to anyway?"

"Wherever *he* went."

"You mean the Magus?"

"The Magus?"

"The one who gave us these collars." Porridge unwound his scarf with a dramatic twirl. "Oh, it's a frightful thing, this. Doesn't match anything I'm wearing!"

"So, he's a Magus," Nox mused.

"Well, that's what he said," Porridge explained. "Not that it wasn't obvious."

"Was it?"

"You don't remember?"

"I've got snippets, but I can't quite tell what's real and what's something the Man with the Silver Mane put in my head. I don't even remember how we got to the Lostlands in the first place, or why."

Porridge cocked an eyebrow. "What's that, peach? The Man with the Silver Mane? Now, there's a mouthful. Oh!" He placed the tips of his fingers over his mouth in feigned abashment.

"He's the one who's behind all this."

"Oh, we'll find him then, sugar. Don't you worry your sweet little noggin. First, though, you relax those cogs in your head and let me do what my old nanna'd call a *spinning*."

Nox grumbled, but he also perked his ears.

"Good. Ready, plum? Let me fill you in on how we got here."

Chapter Eighteen

BEFORE THEY WERE LOST

The strange copter chugged through the skies. It looked kind of like a patchwork submarine. It moved kind of like an injured bird, rising and falling suddenly. It sounded like a broken train. Yeah, that was Porridge's vessel, no doubt about it. He called it the Dandyman.

"Are you sure he came this way?" Nox asked, resting one hand on the glass of one of the globular windows. He kept the other hand grasped around a handle nearby. Muscle memory, and good old-fashioned normal memory, made him hold on all the tighter.

"Well, no, blueberry," Porridge replied, "but as old Rommond would say: *There's nothing certain in this world, but there's one thing certain in war.*"

"*Casualties,*" the Coilhunter quipped, finishing the general's saying. He always did have a saying, just like he always did have a gun. Some folk said a man with a mouth needed a gun, because sooner or later he'd say something someone didn't like. Nox'd met a lot of those men. Many of them were saying nothing now.

"Right you are, hun," Porridge said.

"So you think he's dead?" Nox asked, peering out further to see if he could see Chance Oakley's body in the sand. He wasn't entirely sure why he looked. As if the sand would show him. No, he'd have to dig first. The sand wanted you to know it was a grave.

Even Porridge's sigh was shrill. "Oh, I don't know *what* to think." He seemed like he might faint at the wheel, so Nox gave him a look that'd wake him up real quick. It was that same look he gave when they first met, when Porridge was looting the Coilhunter's monowheel. They'd grown close since then, as close as a lawman and someone who skirted the edge of the law could become. It turned out it was pretty close.

Nox pulled himself up, hearing the glass groan beneath him. It always groaned. The whole copter groaned. Even the spirits of the machines couldn't explain how it was held together. Willpower was one hell of a glue.

"I still don't understand why he came out here," Nox said. He grasped a hold of Porridge's seat as it swung down a track to another window. The entire vessel rotated with it as old engines conked out and new ones kicked in. Propellers died and came alive outside. Why, it was the story of life in one big, old hunk of junk.

"*To find myself,*" Porridge mused. "That's all he said."

"I thought he already did."

"Well, plum, he's a drifter."

"So are we," Nox rasped.

"And here we are," Porridge said, "flying over the Lostlands."

"Findin' *him*, not ourselves."

"But aren't we always looking?"

"I ain't no philosopher," Nox said.

"No, peach, you're not."

"Are we any closer to the location of the distress signal?"

"Closer, yes. Oh, I just hope no one else heard!"

Nox scoffed. "There's no point hopin' that. You can damn well bet they heard."

He thought of who might be listening. The bigger gangs would, of course, if they'd stolen the technology. The Regime certainly would. Maybe even the Resistance. The question wasn't: who had heard? It was: who would act?

"Wait," Nox said. "Somethin' doesn't feel right."

"Oh, don't say that, sweetie. You're giving me the willies. Oh, if only!"

"Park her."

"It's a he."

"Park her!" Nox shouted.

But it was too late. Something struck the vessel like lightning. Except it wasn't lightning. It was a blast from a very big electrical gun.

Chapter Nineteen

WHEN THEY WERE TAKEN

The Dandyman went down, less like an airship careening across the sky, and more like a copper ball plummeting to the earth. Porridge did everything he could to slow the fall. He knew the vessel's weaknesses, and he built around and on top of them. He built it *expecting* it to fall. So he had wind traps, automated schutes, tilting sails, and more. The more kept growing after every scavenge.

But it didn't matter how much Porridge had prepared the vessel. It was still one hell of a hard landing.

The Coilhunter'd banged his head off the rails at the moment of the impact. It wasn't a lot of blood, but it was one mighty concussion. When the robed figures entered, he wasn't just at sixes and sevens. He was at every number and none all at once.

"Is that … the Sandsweeper?" one of the figures asked.

"By God, it is!"

"His Eminence will want to see him."

"Bundle 'im up!"

The last thing Nox heard was the voice of Porridge: "Unhand me, you fiends! Oh! Oh!"

*   *   *

When Nox awoke, he found himself strapped to a table. They hadn't taken his gadgets. They hadn't taken his guns. Even now, with his head still groggy, he made a promise that they'd regret that.

"You're awake," a man said. His voice was deep and old, with more gravel in it than even Nox could muster. That was saying something. Nox could muster a lot.

The Coilhunter said nothing. He was watching. Observing. Studying. You learned to watch your enemy before you slung your gun. That way you knew if they would dive, and where. That way you knew if they would die, and when. You didn't just observe. You captured them in your mind. When you decided to let them go, they'd go with a bullet in their head.

"You resisted the collar," the man said. Nox noted the shimmer around the figure's face. The light caught his long, silver waves of hair and made them sparkle, as if they were only half there, fading in from another realm. Nox was enraptured for a moment, but his own desert training kicked in and told him it was just a mirage. The man shifted, and the light shifted, and it was just grey hair after all.

"I—"

"Don't speak," the man said. "You spent a lot of energy fighting. And without a collar, no less!"

That last part seemed to aggravate his captor more than anything. It didn't seem he minded the struggle. He minded the fact that Nox wasn't yet a slave.

Nox was surprised that he complied. He didn't

speak. Something about this place, or that man, or this collar, made him soft, made him weak. He could barely find the energy to move. No, that wasn't it. He could feel the energy. It was there. He didn't *want* to move.

"You'll make a fine specimen," the man said. It seemed he wasn't quite talking to him, but documenting his experiments out loud. He didn't have to worry that anyone heard. It didn't matter if they heard. He knew they couldn't *act*.

"W—"

"Even now you struggle. It's that determination that makes you valuable. It is *will* that works like magic here. It is *will* that works like Glass."

Glass. Even in his daze, Nox knew that. Glass with a capital G. It was the crystal the Resistance had unearthed in the mines and employed the Magi to enchant. One faction of the Resistance, known simply as the Order, was in charge of production. With it, they made the amulets that supposedly stopped women from giving birth to demon children. The demons were the Regime, of course, but then you couldn't help but paint your enemy with horns.

"I will make a portal yet," the man said. "I am getting close now. Just a few more people like you. Just a dash more willpower. I will harness your minds. Minds are the magicians here."

Someone came in, addressed the man as Your Eminence, and sedated Nox. Things didn't quite go black then, but a kind of grey. No. A kind of silver. He could still see faint silhouettes moving back and forth. He could still hear faint mumbles far off.

Then he heard another sound, but it was louder. "Nox!" the voice called.

It was Chance Oakley.

Chapter Twenty

HOW HE ESCAPED

The voice was like a fishing line, reeling Nox back from the brink. His vision grew crisper, and he could see the silhouettes stronger now. He could hear the voices stronger too. Yes, that was Chance Oakley alright. That warm timbre was familiar. But it was also frantic. There was a lot of fear in that voice.

Nox feigned sleep, and he didn't have to feign much, because he was halfway there. When the silhouettes moved away, he stirred. They didn't even chain him to the bed. They didn't have to. They were so confident that he would comply, that he would be just another slave. But the Coilhunter hadn't just honed his body. He'd honed his mind. To do real good, you needed both. Now he needed both to just get out of there alive.

He had a sense for presence, which helped when he needed to turn quickly and get his shot in before the gunslinger behind him. Here, it helped him know when the folk in the room left. He knew the silver-haired man was gone, because his presence was stronger. His presence was like that of ten men. Nox made a mental note of it, because he knew he'd have to come back for him.

Nox got to his feet, but his legs wobbled. The drugs they'd given him were potent, enough to dull and weaken him. But there was something they should've known. He was the Coilhunter. They should've given him more.

He hobbled across to the doorway. His eyes were adjusting, but they weren't adjusting fast enough. It was lucky he'd previously fought silhouettes when his light bombs went off before he had a chance to put on his goggles. He'd gotten used to fighting shapes of men, and gotten used to feeling for the presence of them to distinguish the good from the bad. In the Wild North, you got used to that quick, or you got used to the grave.

He ventured out into the hallway, hugging the wall. He passed by a room of many prone silhouettes. He could see other figures attaching collars to them. Part of him wanted to fight them now, but he knew he had to play this tactfully. He had to learn what he could. He had to get out alive and let those drugs wear off. He had to come back stronger.

There was one figure pacing the hall in front of him. Behind, there were several more approaching. Nox couldn't quite tell if the person ahead had his back turned, but he presumed he did by the fact that he didn't shout or run. Nox stalked up to him as quietly as he could. As he did, he thumbed a butterfly capsule from his belt, unscrewed it, and plucked one of the spring-loaded mechanical butterflies from inside. They normally exploded into action when the timer released, but Nox didn't feel like alerting everyone with a corridor full of butterflies. One would do the job just fine. He swiftly wrapped his arm around the man's mouth, pressing the butterfly against his lips. It released its gas, and the man slumped to the ground. Nox dragged the body behind a table.

Nox continued on. He slunk around corners, skirted into alcoves, and hid in abandoned rooms. He made himself just another shadow on the wall as guards and scientists passed. Sure, some of them looked over their shoulders. You see, most had heard of the Coilhunter. They knew to be scared of shadows.

He heard a commotion far behind him and knew that the alarm'd been raised about his disappearance. Now he knew he couldn't just escape quietly. He'd have to fight his way out.

It was then that he passed a room with an electrical generator. A silhouette with a clipboard stood nearby, assessing the machinery. As Nox creeped in, he smelled something charred. He ran his fingers across the wall, feeling the scorch marks. Electricity was new to the world of Altadas, and more of an experiment than a reliable source of power. Nox'd made his own tests with it, but he hadn't yet managed to generate large enough quantities. Here, they had. But it was unstable. And it was just the kind of thing he could use to escape.

Nox quietly felt along the floor for wires and pulled up one of the loose ones. He could hear, and feel, the crackle of energy at the end. It was powerful. No wonder the silver-haired man worked with it.

"I don't understand," the scientist told himself, tapping a pen off the clipboard in agitation. "It should be stronger than this. It should be—"

Nox jammed the open wire into the man's back, jolting him. He fell, his hair sizzling. Nox could still see him breathing, but boy would he wake up frazzled.

"Seems pretty strong enough," Nox said.

Two figures raced into the room just as Nox slid behind the door.

"What in—?"

"Howdy." Nox jabbed them with the wire, then dragged their bodies into a pile. No one would've ever accused him of being *neat* with his work, per se, but there was something about a pile of bodies that spoke wonders to the bad. Especially if there was room for more.

Nox waited for his eyes to adjust further, but his vision was still strained. He started to see some things clearer, but there were white spots on his vision, and his eyes were extremely sensitive to the light of the electric-powered lanterns nearby. What surprised Nox was how dim they were. They weren't generating this much power for lights. They were saving it for something else. Something bigger.

He moved back and forth between the generator, where he inspected the wiring and controls, and the door, where he added another body or two to the pile. He was making quite a collection. But there was still space at the top for the mastermind of all this.

He could've spent hours, or days, analysing the machinery. He would've liked to discover how they generated this much electricity without the entire place being torn apart. Of course, he could see the scorch marks more clearly. He could only imagine that his pile of bodies wasn't the first one in there.

Many died for science. Many more died for madness. Sometimes they just exchanged the labels.

But someone was approaching. Nox initially thought to run to the door, to add another body to the pile, but already he could feel him. Already he could feel the presence. This was the silver-haired man.

He entered the room, and Nox already had a pistol on him. The man seemed unfazed, and this was the first time the Coilhunter got a real good look at him. He had a distinct silhouette, partly due to his tall-crowned pilgrim hat, black as death, partly due to his larger, almost artificially pointed nose, and partly due to his long, thick locks of glinting, grey hair. Around him, around his oddly puffed black clothing, around his silhouette, there was a kind of haze. The kind you see in the shimmering heat. If this was a mirage, it was one hell of an illusion. And if it was a mirage, it was one that could talk.

"Quite a mess you made here."

Nox was tired and weak, but that didn't stop his reply. "You should see what I do to you."

"Your threats mean nothing to me."

"Well, what do my bullets mean?"

"Living here has dulled me to your words. Even if you killed me now, it would be an escape. Don't you see? That's all I want, Coilhunter. Escape."

Nox clicked the hammer. "Well, hows about I open the door then?"

"What is it *you* want, Coilhunter?"

"*My* escape," Nox replied. "For now."

"But you're a part of the puzzle. A part of the machine."

"Well, people lose parts all the time."

"I need to complete my work. It is a great work, one that will be remembered."

"Oh, I'll remember it alright."

"You need to stay and be a part of it."

"You need to back down, pilgrim. You need to give this up and let these folk free."

Nox felt a sudden jolt of electricity around his neck. He saw the silver-haired man's finger on a button. He heard the screams and moans of others who received that same electric lash.

"You're not just hurting yourself, Coilhunter. You're hurting them."

Nox moved the gun towards the generator. "Well, hows about I put us all out of our misery?"

"You wouldn't dare."

"Oh, you don't know what I'd do."

"It'd kill us all."

"Well, it'd end this, sure."

"You're bluffing."

Nox told himself he wasn't. He told himself he believed it. He told himself he'd do it. He didn't just lie to his enemy. For this moment of guile, he had to lie to himself. He had to make them see in his eyes that he meant it. He thought of his family and how dying would mean he got to join them. His finger dangled on the trigger. "Am I?"

They stared each other down for a moment, even as more guards and scientists entered. The silver-haired man stopped them from advancing, from sending the Coilhunter over the edge, and all of them into oblivion. He wanted his escape, but not like this.

Not after all this work. Not after all this pain. He had his own family to go back to.

"Wait," the man said.

"Oh, I'm waitin'."

"You may leave, on one condition."

"I'll leave *in* one condition," Nox said. "Alive and well."

"You must come back."

Nox smirked. "Didn't you know that was a given?"

"In Altadas, there is only one given."

"Death," Nox said. "And that's what I meant."

"You will return then."

"Oh, I'll return."

The silver-haired man paused for a moment, then ushered his men away. "We'll clear a path for you. You can follow the lights out."

"How do I know you won't just try to kill or cage me?"

"Because I'm a man of my word, Coilhunter. It's how I know you'll return. Because you're a man of your word too."

"Well, there ain't no bluffin' there."

"Until next time, Coilhunter."

The man left, and the presence left with him. When it was far enough away, Nox almost collapsed to the ground. He'd been bluffing alright, and he'd been bluffing strength. There was only so long he could keep that poker face up. Sooner or later they'd see that grim determination turn into a grimace.

He hobbled out into the corridor and followed the lights. They'd doused lanterns along other passages he wasn't to follow, and part of him felt like probing the darkness there. He could feel another presence down one hallway, but he knew he hadn't the strength to face it. He had to regroup, even if it was a group of one.

He reached a door, which was already open for him. It was dark outside, but they'd lit lanterns along the cracked path down from the fortress. He made a mental note of it, drew an X on the map of his mind. He'd come back, sure enough, just like the silver-haired man said, but he'd come back in force.

He wandered across the desert until he could no longer see the pinnacle of the castle of sand. The last he saw of that place was its far-off silhouette when a bolt of lightning seemed to crackle off its tip. Then he kept going, until exhaustion mixed with the drugs and made their own sleep-inducing cocktail. He faded off then, and the memory of what'd happened started to fade with him. He tried to grasp at it, tried to fire a grapnel at it, but it slipped through his fingers of flesh and those fingers of metal. All that was left was the presence. As things turned black, Nox promised himself that'd be enough.

Chapter Twenty-one

FINDING YOUR PLACE

"So, that's how it happened, pickle," Porridge said. He gave a series of little bows to an imagined audience, then struck a pose, resting his elbow on his other arm, with hand aloft, fingers dangling.

"So, that's how it happened," the Coilhunter mused.

"You really don't remember?"

"I remember more of it now, now that you've jolted my memory." And it was quite the jolt. As Porridge told his tale, Nox recalled chunks of his own adventure, of how he'd been caught, and how he'd escaped. Quite the jolt indeed.

"Like lightning," Porridge quipped.

"Hmm. Like lightnin'."

"Of course, for me it wasn't quite so adventurous," Porridge explained. "I convinced the Lost Tribe to take me in. It didn't take a lot of convincing. I promised them access to powerful machinery, to poor old Bitnickle. And, and, well—"

"And?"

"And, well, of course, *your* machinery too."

"Well, colour me surprised."

"Oh, that's not a colour that suits you, love."

"Well, then colour me angry."

"Oh! Now, that's more familiar."

Nox smirked.

"So, what'll we do now, plum?" Porridge asked. He pawed at Nox's shoulder.

"Well, we won't dress up like tribesmen, that's for sure."

"That was genuine top class survival, that was," Porridge said with a humph.

Nox smiled, but said nothing. He'd gotten pretty used to smiling beneath the mask, and folk had gotten pretty used to seeing the smile in his eyes instead—if they didn't just see the hurt and the hate. You lived for the little moments, the passing smiles, because you never knew how many of them you'd get. In the Wild North, most never got enough.

"You never did ask," Porridge said solemnly after some silent stomping.

"What's that?"

"About where I came from, cabbage."

"I thought you didn't have a home."

"Well, I don't, plum, at least not how you see it."

"Tell me then."

"Hmm?"

"Tell me where you came from."

"Here, sweetheart."

Nox halted. He didn't mean to halt, but sometimes the only way for your mind to move forward was for your feet to stop first. "Here? You mean the Lostlands."

"Yes, plum. Oh! It brings back memories."

"Does it now? Funny thing, that, the sand."

"Well, as you know, honey, you tend to get a feel

for the sand the more you live in it. Oh! A feel! Umm. The tribes have many words for it, for the red sands, for the yellow, even for these seemingly coarser grains up here. And oh! It does bring back memories."

"Keep talkin' then," Nox said. He knew Porridge wanted to, but needed a little encouragement, a little acknowledgement that he was being listened to. It reminded him of dearest Emma, Nox' one and only beloved, and one of only three people he truly loved. She needed that encouragement and acknowledgement too. After she passed, he felt he hadn't ever given her enough. They say you always regret what you never did. That was why he became the Coilhunter, the Man with the Thousand Names, because he knew otherwise he'd have a thousand regrets to go with them. Nox sighed. It seemed the sand was bringing back memories too. There was a different one in every grain.

"My people were always wanderers," Porridge explained. "Always tinkers and scavengers. *Waste not, want not*, as the saying goes. Oh, dear old dandy Rommond has a saying too: *Use it while you can and speak it while you can*. Well, to us, to my family, the discarded spoke things that the people discarding them never ever heard. We accepted the refuse, the unwanted, the unloved. We gave them a place, plum, and a purpose."

"Like Oddcopper and Bitnickle," Nox said. Those two clockwork constructs were refugees of sorts from the Rust Valley, from the ravenous, human-flaying horde of the Clockwork Commune. They were two little mechanical creatures, more alive and sentient than the ones the Coilhunter made. They escaped the terrors of their scrapyard home and lived with the scrap in Porridge's copter. They helped him salvage, and they found their place in the world.

They were partners of sorts, in their own unusual way, just like Nox and Porridge were, in their even more unusual way. Yet, after a time, those two little constructs fell apart. Oddcopper wanted to settle down. Bitnickle wanted to have adventures. So Oddcopper went back to Nox and stayed in his workshop, helping him build things, painting a little smile of joy on his face after each successful creation. Bitnickle stayed with Porridge, going on adventures in the sky, in the sea, and just about everywhere else. They saw each other again when Nox and Porridge met. They were shy to show it, but it was a joyful reunion.

"Oh, don't remind me!" Porridge exclaimed. He was a hopeless romantic and hated seeing those little constructs apart. He kept trying to usher them back together, but Bitnickle always spoke of having a greater purpose. She spoke it with her radio, switching channels to make up her speech. "Poor little plum and peach. Oh!"

"You were sayin'," Nox rasped.

"I was, wasn't I? Oh, plonk a colourful hat on my head or I'll lose it! Oh! Where was I? Oh, yes. We were a family, and I say that in a loose way, because we weren't just a family of blood. We welcomed others in. We grew. We saw them as our brothers and sisters, as our uncles and aunts. If they felt at home with us, well, sugar, they didn't need a home."

"Your own kind of Lost Tribe," Nox mused.

"Yes, I guess so, blueberry. And that's the thing. You had to be lost to find us. We were a family that found our purpose here in the emptiness. That's one of the reasons why others come out here, why Chance came out here. Most never do find their purpose, but I did."

"And what's that?" Nox asked. Oh, he'd found his own purpose long ago. His family's death gave him a purpose. The Wild North gave him a mission.

"To journey," Porridge said. "To wander and not be lost."

"A true drifter."

"Yes, but more than just a passing thing, plum. It's about making everything a passing thing. Like the sand. You don't bother making a house there, because you know it'll blow away. So you make yourself tumbleweed. You roll with the wind. You see where it takes you."

"And what if it's not anywhere good?"

"Well, I try not to judge the journey, peach. There are lessons to be learned and experiences to be had in all stops along the way. The good *and* the bad."

"And the ugly?"

Porridge beamed. "Oh, now, plum, show me someone ugly and let me do my magic on him. Oh, he'll come out all dashing and dandy. Oh! If he ever comes out at all!"

They continued on for a time, following the trail until it grew faint with the fading light, then farther until it grew a little clear again in moonlight. In time, they halted, spotting what looked like the silhouette of an orb on the horizon.

"Your copter," Nox assumed, though he wished he'd made the assumption in his head. That way, if you were wrong, you didn't look like a fool. And that way, if you were wrong, the land didn't try to teach you a harsh lesson. Well, you could count on something: it was always learning time.

"My baby!" Porridge screamed, starting into a trot, which quickly led to a bumbling gallop.

"Wait," Nox said, but nothing could stop Porridge steamrolling ahead. And boy did he roll. He went head over heels down a dune, but was off again, almost as lithely as the Coilhunter was when he was dodging bullets.

They got closer, close enough to see the copper plating on the Dandyman glinting in the sunlight. Close enough to see the damaged propellers and the embers of dying engines. Close enough to see members of the Lost Tribe working their repairs— and now grabbing their rifles.

Chapter Twenty-two

MAKING IT HOME

The first hail of bullets sent Porridge into the dirt, screaming. He clutched at his scarves and rolled about in the sand, his arms flailing.

"I'm hit! Oh, my ripened raspberries, I'm down! Oh!"

Nox raced over, rolling and sliding through the sand. He lobbed a smoke canister towards the copter, which exploded into a thick, grey haze.

"Where'd they get you?" Nox asked. He tried to find the wound, but Porridge patted his hands away.

"Leave me, Nox. Oh! Oh, just leave me to die, poor old dandy that I am. Oh!"

Nox finally swatted Porridge's hands away to find a bullet had slightly grazed the man's chest. It'd done more damage to his blouse, and Nox had a feeling that'd hurt more.

"Nox!" Porridge cried, clinging to the Coilhunter's arm. "I see stars, plum. Stars!"

Nox glanced up at the night sky, where, indeed, the stars were shining bright.

"You'll be fine," he said. He dropped Porridge's arm and stood up to face the tribesfolk. He knew for certain they wouldn't be.

* * *

The tribesfolk circled the area slowly, spreading out. All guns pointed in towards the slowly fading smoke. They could've fired in, like Regime soldiers would've, but that would've been a waste of ammunition, which was in short supply out here in the Lostlands, where even the most enterprising traders never went. No. You did what the Coilhunter would've done. You saved your shots.

Except that's not what the Coilhunter did.

They saw something emerge from the smoke at a lightning pace, so they turned and fired at it. It banged in response. But it wasn't the Masked Menace. It was just a small metal box: a noisemaker, which rattled out the sounds of gunfire.

The Masked Menace came after, and he came from the other side. He leaped up and out of the haze, and he came with the swing of a newly-fired grappling gun. The grapple took the tribesmen's feet like a flail, toppling two and injuring another. Then Nox turned sharply and swung the weapon again. The hook caught one of the fallen men who was just standing up and sliced into his leg. Nox yanked hard, pulling him down again before it unhooked back into the launcher.

Another tribesman fired from the left, but Nox dodged and ducked. He fired the grapple again, straight into the tribesman's face. He heard the crunch of the jaw breaking, and wondered what else he'd have to break before that man learned his lesson. For the law breakers, he'd have no trouble teaching them with bullets. But these were not altogether bad men. Just foolish men. Real foolish for challenging the Coilhunter.

One more rifle came from the right, but it was close. Nox dashed forward and kicked it up. The bullet fired off into the sky. Then the Coilhunter grabbed the barrel, pulled it from side to side, and then pushed it back suddenly before swiping with the butt of the gun against the attacker's face. Even as he did this, he heard the stirring of leather behind him, and the click of a hammer. He turned sharply, falling to one knee, and fired. His bullet blasted the gun out of the other tribesman's hand, and almost blasted away the hand as well.

Nox got up and strolled over. He pointed the rifle right between the man's eyes.

"Now," Nox said. "Don't you go startin' fights you ain't gonna win."

The man started to plead. "This is … we only—"

Nox brought the gun down until the man was mouthing around the barrel. "Let me finish," he said. "Don't you go startin' fights at all. Y'hear?"

"D-d-don't kill me," the man pleaded, nudging the barrel away with one gentle finger. He had to be gentle, because he wanted the Coilhunter to be gentle too. They say "no sudden movements" for a reason. The most sudden movement for many was the click of a gun.

"I won't if you tell your friend here to stay down," Nox said, nodding towards one of the other tribesmen, who was starting to stand up. The tribesmen exchanged nervous glances before the second man laid back down again. The other men, nursing wounds and fear, never even tried to stand. Not when the Sandsweeper was there to sweep you back off your feet.

"One more request," Nox said, though they knew damn well that it was an order. "Your leader. Rassa-somethin'."

"Rassa-tu—"

"Let. Me. Finish."

The tribesman shivered as the black smoke exploded from Nox's mask.

"Where can I find 'im? Or, better yet, where can I find *his* master?"

The tribesman shivered again, but this time was different. Nox could see the horror of a memory in his eyes.

"The castle," the man whispered.

"The castle?"

"The castle of sand."

"And where's that?"

The man nudged himself up onto his elbows and glanced around. It seemed like he was just about to point a finger when a dart whizzed by, piercing him straight in the forehead. He spasmed for a moment from the poison, then fell limp. There was a flurry among the other tribesfolk as they clambered up and tried to run, but all of them fell to the same darts. It took a moment for the Coilhunter to realise he'd also been pierced by one, but before he fully felt the effects, he pulled an antidote syringe from his belt and jabbed it into his leg. Normally it was the sting of a scorpion or the bite of a desert snake. Of course, normally he wasn't in the Lostlands.

Nox looked for the attacker, spotting Rassa standing close to the copter with a blowpipe held to his mouth. Three other tribesmen stood nearby with similar weapons aimed. They fired a final volley at the Coilhunter, but he dodged them quick. Not that it mattered. The antivenom would inoculate him for now.

Nox ran for the blowgunners, and they ran too. One paused to fire another dart at Nox, which struck him square in the shoulder. Nox didn't even try to evade that one. He just yanked it free and flicked it away like it was a mosquito. Then he caught up with his attacker, exchanged blows, and smashed the tribesman's head against the hull of the Dandyman. That vessel was good for all sorts.

Nox heard Rassa shouting in his broken tribal tongue to men inside the copter. Some of them raced out, but Nox could see through the bubble windows as others worked furiously inside on the repairs. It seemed like the scavenger's vehicle was being scavenged.

Nox circled the copter, ready for a gunfight or a fistfight, or, well, any kind of fight. He halted, spotting Rassa climbing onto a monowheel. No. *Into* one. And not just any monowheel. This was the Coilhunter's vehicle, right down to the bounty box at the back. But it was different. Oh, it still had the big outer wheel augmented with landship treads. But it also had glass bubbles on the side. Windows from the Dandyman. They combined on either side to make the vessel into a ball.

Rassa gave a derisive wave before the glass sealed shut. Then he rolled off, safe inside his bubble, safe from Nox's grapnel and safe from his guns. No wonder he was smug.

Well, Rassa should've known it wouldn't be that easy.

Chapter Twenty-three

COPPER TUMBLEWEED

When the Coilhunter entered the Dandyman, some of the tribesmen working on the repairs fled at the sight of him. Others tried to fight, but Nox made quick work of them, adding their bodies to the debris and salvage littered across the interior. He dragged the bodies to one of the empty windows, where Rassa's men had removed the glass, and lobbed them outside. Normally he'd be bringing the bodies back with him to the Bounty Booth. But Nox only wanted one bounty now.

Porridge stood at the door, clasping the edge for support. Turned out he'd survived the blouse wound after all. "Oh, they've made such a mess!"

Nox couldn't help but raise an eyebrow. It was always a mess. What he couldn't help more was the urge to get the copter moving before Rassa got too far away.

"Get it started," Nox barked to Porridge. He didn't mean to bark, but boy did those tribesmen bring out the animal in him. Some said there were totem animals for all the folk of the Wild North. If that were true, then the Coilhunter's was something big. And something frightening.

"Oh, I don't think I can, pumpkin!"

Nox looked at him intently. "I *know* you can."

The tinker pranced between the debris. He yanked a lever here and there and bashed his fist against a whole lot of buttons. Then he slouched into the driver's seat, flipped his scarf over his shoulder, and prodded the controls.

"Hmm," he said, and tried again.

"I hope that's a *hmm, it's workin'*."

"It's *working*, dearie, yes, but ..." Porridge pointed at indicator lights on the dashboard, close to a crudely drawn icon of an engine. "Five engines out." He pointed to another set of lights beside a propeller icon. "And six propellers. Oh!"

"Ain't that ... normal?" Nox asked. He was used to the vessel not so much as *flying* as rolling across the sky, with one set of engines and propellers conking out, and another set kicking in just in time. The entire vessel would rotate then, and the driver's seat would roll along its track to the next window and set of controls. It was a kind of copper tumbleweed, drifting across the desert sky.

"It won't fly," Porridge said, his arms drooping over the armrests in exaggerated resignation. "Oh! What are we to do, peach? Oh!"

Nox let out a long, deep sigh. The kind of sigh that came with a long trail of black smoke from his mask. The kind of sigh that he'd given far too many times before when criminals narrowly escaped his grasp. He turned and rested an arm on one of the protruding iron beams above.

"Porridge," Nox said. "Forget about flyin'."

"But sweetie!"

"Roll it."

Porridge turned to him, incredulous.

"Roll it like a ball," Nox said. "Like a marble."

"I … I'm not sure if I can, blueberry."

"Again," Nox said, giving him that keen look once more. "I *know* you can."

Porridge bit his lip. "Oh, you better hang on then, plum!"

Nox clutched the back of the pilot's chair.

"Tighter, dear!" Porridge urged. "Oh! Always tighter, umm."

He fired up the working engines and turned on the propellers. Outside, they spun wildly, some of them scooping up the sand that'd built up around the hull of the Dandyman. The vessel budged, but it didn't roll.

"There's too much sand!" Porridge cried. "Oh! We're drowning in it!"

Nox let go of the pilot's chair, grabbed a piece of salvage, and strolled over to the bodies outside. Several of the tribesmen had already stirred, but all were still nursing their wounds. Some were nursing them in their sleep. The waking ones flinched at the sight of the Coilhunter.

"You boys," Nox rasped. "You work for me now."

The tribesmen looked at each other, confused.

"This," Nox said, holding up the scrap piece. By the looks of it, it was a piece of an engine, but boy, it didn't look like much. "This is a new pet of mine."

He could already see their eyes widen. They knew his pets, or they'd heard of them. Sometimes the tales were worse than reality. Sometimes in the stories, Owl had fangs and Duck had teeth.

"He's a," Nox said, pausing to inspect the item, "mouse." If you looked at the piece from the right angle, it almost looked like one. You really did have to look hard though. Luckily enough, imagination was a powerful thing.

"Now," Nox continued. "D'ya wanna find out what he does?"

They shook their heads frantically. Of course they didn't. They already knew what many of his other toys did. They blinded you. They knocked you out. They caught you and they killed you. This one was just a mouse. What could it do? There was a reason the elephants were scared.

The Coilhunter cast the scrap-turned-mouse near the tribesmen, and they flinched more than if he'd drawn a gun. He went back into the Dandyman and emerged with three shovels. He tossed one, then the remaining two together.

"Now, you dig 'round the copter. You dig us out, y'hear?"

They didn't protest, even though they wanted to.

"I'll let *him* keep an eye on ya. Oh, and he'll be watchin' close. Now, don't you go pettin' 'im, boys, even though he likes it. You don't wanna get 'im … excited."

Nox turned back to the Dandyman.

"I have no shovel," one of the tribesmen protested. It was a quiet protest, almost a silent one.

"You've got your hands," Nox said. "For now."

Nox strolled back inside and tapped his belt,

where he had a real mechanical mouse waiting. He knew what that one did just fine.

Back inside the Dandyman, Porridge was working furiously at the controls. Nox found his way to one of the engine rooms and removed several panels for inspection. The wiring was so patchwork, it might as well've been sewn together by a child. They criss-crossed over each other, blocking access to other vital machinery. Porridge might've had a way of making things work, but that didn't mean it was the right way.

"Some job you've done back here," Nox grumbled.

"Is Bitnickle there?" Porridge asked. "She can help."

"No. I don't see her."

"Oh! I hope she's okay!"

"Worry about us for now."

Nox worked more furiously than Porridge, pulling tools from his belt to fix the engine and remove some debris jamming the cogs controlling the propeller outside. When the engine was up and running, he shovelled coal with gunslinger speed. He glanced from time to time to his new employees outside, who shovelled a little furiously too. Nox swore that all of this would pale compared to the fury the Man with the Silver Mane would feel.

"I've got it!" Porridge shouted, but he didn't need to shout. The Coilhunter could already feel the rumble. The copter shifted suddenly. The propellers weren't just scooping up sand now. They were acting like oars, moving the vessel. Then, just as quickly, they were acting like wheels.

Porridge's voice echoed. "Grab a hold of

something! Oh!"

Nox grabbed what he could to hold himself in place.

The Dandyman rolled forward.

It was a controlled roll. One propeller nudged it this way, and the vessel rotated until another propeller caught against the sand and pushed it the other way. It wasn't far off how Porridge flew it in the air. As they tumbled, Nox couldn't help but visualise his son playing marbles in the dirt. Little wild Aaron. Oh, how he'd fire those marbles, and how he'd collected more. But now Nox visualised the prized marble for his own collection. The one with Rassa in it.

Chapter Twenty-four

MARBLES

The Dandyman rolled, and it was gaining ground. The propellers worked like wheels, but more than anything, it was gravity that helped. The entire vessel plunged down dunes, picking up speed. It swung up steep climbs, spinning into the air before crashing down into another roll. Porridge steered it as best he could, knocking out a propeller if he didn't want it to push or pull, and firing up another to help the ball tumble into a turn. He was a natural at fixing the unfixable and making the unworkable work, at making the unflyable fly—at making the unmoveable move. And boy did it move.

"How are you hanging in back there, cabbage?" Porridge shouted. His pilot seat sailed around the rails, keeping him upright. It was the exact opposite of the Coilhunter's monowheel. For that, the outer wheel rotated, and the driver stayed put.

"Barely!" Nox grunted in response. His head was dizzy as he pressed his limbs against the hull. The vessel tumbled, so he tumbled. There was no rail to keep him upright, no seat to keep him in place.

He had to steady his nerves and focus his mind. He imagined himself upright, placed himself in the cactus field of his mind, readying for the draw and the kill. It was something he'd learned to do in the years after his family's death. One by one, his bullets punched holes in the cacti. In time, he'd replace the desert plants with people. Conmen. Criminals. The bad. The Wanted. He'd practice his shots in his mind just as much as in the land around him. That way he could guarantee his kills.

Once he'd focused enough, he switched to a mental map of the Dandyman. He'd been there often enough to know it well, though Porridge had a habit of moving things around. *There's no one place for me*, he'd say, *so why should there be one spot for them?* Of course, *them* could be anything. When Nox first met him, it was his monowheel. Now someone else was trying to steal it.

When the moment felt right, Nox opened his eyes and hoisted himself out into the main chamber, firing his right grapnel immediately. Barely a second later, as the hook latched into place, he fired his left grapnel in the opposite direction. The wires went taut, holding him in place, dangling and spinning in the centre of the vessel. Then, just as Porridge's pilot chair sailed underneath him, he released the grapnels, dropped down, and quickly grabbed the chair.

Porridge blew him a kiss. "Nice of you to join me, peach."

Nox's head still swam. It was enough to make him almost lose his grip, but he told himself that the edge of the pilot's chair was the handle of his gun. He told himself that because he knew then he wouldn't let go. When he steadied himself enough, he noticed the loose straps on the back of Porridge's chair and used them to secure himself in place.

Outside, the marbles continued to roll. The monowheel was faster, but the bulk of the Dandyman meant that gravity pulled it down all the quicker when the path turned into a slope. The inclines were harder, but Porridge had a way of making it work. He didn't leave things to chance either. He gambled on losing. The whole vessel was a testament to that. It had a lot of backup propellers to help steer the way.

In time, they came close to Rassa's vehicle, close enough that they could've struck if the Dandyman wasn't carrying so much scavenged material. But close wasn't good enough. The chase didn't mean anything if it wasn't followed by the catch.

"Oh, that reminds me, plum. I've made a … modification." Porridge nodded towards a heavy lever on the control panel. "Give that a good thug, will you, dear? Oh, if only!"

Nox complied. Outside, a mechanical arm unfolded from the centre of the hull, rotating on its own axis so as to stay upright throughout the vessel's tumbles. The Coilhunter could see it dangling over the desert terrain outside.

"Well don't just stand there gawking!" Porridge exclaimed. He nodded to a control stick. "You can move it with that knob there. Oh!"

Nox moved the arm around, getting a good feel for it. He couldn't see it quite as clearly from most of the windows he was forced to look out of as the pilot's chair sailed around the ball, but what glimpses he got were enough to gauge how far he needed to move it.

Nox almost had Rassa's vehicle in the grasp of the mechanical arm, but at the last moment, he paused, letting Rassa roll away.

"Nox! You're letting him get away!"

"No," Nox said. "I'm lettin' him *lead* the way. I ain't no bettin' man, but if I were, I'd wager he's headin' back to his master."

"And you want him to go?"

"I want to catch 'im on the doorstep."

"Then why even chase, sugar?"

"'Cause he needs to feel he's at risk of gettin' caught. He needs to know how close we are, that he needs to do desperate things to get away."

"Oh, and what if he really *does* do desperate things? Like die! Or kill! Oh!"

"We won't let 'im."

They continued on further, following the zig-zagging trail Rassa left behind. He was desperate alright. He was trying hard to shake them. He was trying harder now that the long mechanical arm of the law had almost caught him.

Then, after one more steep climb, Rassa's marble came to a halt.

"What's he doing?" Porridge asked.

Nox shook his head. *He can't be givin' up. Not yet.* Maybe he'd realised what the Coilhunter wanted, that he was chasing him all the way home. Maybe he thought it better to give up now than give up his life for leading the Coilhunter back to the castle of sand. Or maybe he was just getting ready to fight. Well, you could bet your life on *maybes*. Nox bet the lives of the bad on *sure and certain*.

The Dandyman rolled up cautiously to the monowheel. Porridge parked it just feet away. Yeah, those marbles hadn't quite clinked together yet. Neither one could claim the prize.

Then, as Nox and Porridge shifted their eyes from Rassa to where that tribesman stared, they realised why he halted. They saw it. A sand fortress on the horizon, with a pinnacle bursting with periodic blasts of lightning. They were close now. Close enough that they could smell the diesel from the monowheel. Close enough that they could almost see the sweat upon Rassa's brow.

Then their eyes travelled down and they saw the immense valley before the castle, with its many sand pits and winding paths, a deadly maze of sand-swept features. Except it *wasn't* a valley. No, this was something carved from the earth. This was something crafted by man. This was an arena.

Chapter Twenty-five

OUT OF WATER

Elsewhere in the Lostlands, other things stirred. The burrows opened, and out came the desert rodents. The snakes made patterns in the sand. The scorpions scuttled across the dunes. The dung beetles rolled their own brown marbles.

Near a pile of scrap, near the broken and discarded diesel canister of the Coilhunter's monowheel, a toy lay half-submerged in sand. The desert creatures never approached it. They could see it watching, even though it seemed like maybe it was half-asleep.

Then, as night fell, Duck awoke.

He was just a little mechanical toy, an invention to aid the fight against the criminals of the Wild North. Yet some said he was something more. Some called him Mr. Quacky. Some called him the Toy with a Thousand Eyes, even though he only ever had two—those pasted-on eyes. They looked up now at the starlit sky, with its thousand eyes looking back down at him.

It was hard to get upright, as the blast had knocked him onto his back. He'd lost one of his small front wheels, which he used to roll or waddle. It was just a wheel, but to someone or something else, it might as well've been a leg. Duck wondered what it was like for the other legless creatures of the world. He wondered if it was like this. Or that's how some thought he wondered. Maybe he didn't wonder anything at all.

After a long time rocking back and forth, he rolled onto his belly and nudged himself upright. He hobbled forward, then tilted over, and began the struggle again. He did this many times, until he adjusted his weight a little more, using the little springs and cogs inside him to pull his back wheel round to the side for a little stability. That was the thing about Nox's toys. He didn't just make them. He taught them things. He taught them to adapt.

Duck travelled the desert, searching for his master. Maybe "master" wasn't the right word. Maybe it should've been "creator." Maybe, just maybe, it should've been "God." There were many who wandered the desert looking for him. Duck stumbled across the bones of some of them. He remembered his own bones, those little copper and brass pieces. He remembered how his creator stared at them through an eyeglass, and how it seemed like Duck saw a tear through the other side.

Duck was an aquatic beast, and Altadas was the opposite of an aquatic world. There was a time when Nathaniel made toy ducks just like him, when there was a lot more water in the world, back before the Regime came. *Nathaniel*. Yes, that was his name then. So, God had a name. But then he had a thousand names. Now he went by Nox. Now he went by Coilhunter. Duck came after the name Nathaniel died. Duck was the product of a vengeful God.

He waddled on, approaching the desert wildlife. He came to the snake and asked him: *Have you seen the Coilhunter?* The snake said no. He came to the scorpion and asked him: *Have you seen the Sandsweeper?* The scorpion said no. Or, again, that's how it might've seemed if anyone was watching. Maybe if a child was watching. Told you imagination was a powerful thing.

Duck remembered the hours his maker spent on him. Who could say that of men? No. They'd forgotten their source, and that was one of the things that made them bad. But then there were others who paid too much heed to their supposed source, and they were bad too. Maybe the God-fearing and the Godless were still the same: all too human.

Duck wondered what it would be like to be human, or so some humans thought he wondered. Why didn't humans wonder what it would be like to be Duck? Maybe he was a philosophical creature. The only thing he knew, if he knew anything, was that Nox had laboured long and hard. Even though he was designed with vengeance in mind, Nox couldn't help but pour a lot of love into Duck. It was the love he still had left for his family, the love he hadn't gotten to fully show them. He modelled Duck on the old toys, the playthings, the joythings.

Then he put a bomb inside.

The Northfolk grew to fear Duck pretty early on, though many still thought he was just a rumour. They knew Nox was good at putting out phantoms, at making literal and figurative scarecrows. Some feared Duck because of the stories of how the Coilhunter appeared after the explosion of light. Some said the Masked Menace revealed his true form then, that he was more terrifying than any demon.

And some had no time for fear. Some just wondered if Duck was really at home in a desert. Was he lost? Was he always searching for water? Was he always searching for home? Indeed, did Nox spend some of his hours of labour crafting a little lake for him? Did he teach him to swim?

But the ones who wondered such things, and put those imaginary thoughts into his head, weren't the ones Duck was made for. He was made for the other ones, the ones with evil eyes. He was made to make them blind.

So he kept on waddling, on and on, across the emptiness of the desert. He kept searching. He kept hunting. After all, that's what Nox'd do.

Chapter Twenty-six

THE ARENA ABOVE

R assa didn't wait long to admire the way. As much as they could see the fear in his eyes at facing this obstacle course, he feared more being dragged into the Bounty Booth. He knew the Coilhunter usually dragged you in dead. He fired up the engine again and dropped down the long, steep slope into the valley of holes, traps, and God-knows-what-else. If God knew, he wasn't telling. Or maybe he was trapped there as well.

Porridge accelerated soon after, letting gravity be his pedal. The Dandyman tumbled down after Rassa's marble, rolling maybe a little too quick. The slope seemed to grow steeper, almost vertical, and the arena just begged you to come down too fast, to turn too slow. Those were big mistakes. But then so was entering at all.

Rassa's monowheel skidded into a turn near the first dark pit. You wouldn't have even known it was a drop but for the lanterns around the edge. Even in the heat of the moment, Nox wondered whose job it was to come out here and light all those. Well, the Man with the Silver Mane didn't employ anyone. He had slaves.

Porridge scrambled with the controls to slow his vessel. It clipped the edge of the pit, knocking a lantern down into the depths. The light hurtled down a long way before the darkness swallowed it. The land was playing marbles now, and it was playing to win.

The Dandyman chased the monowheel between the zig-zagging lanterns, which marked deep drops on either side. The chase continued down a spiralling path, which led through a tunnel and back out into a lower plain. There, statues of cobras didn't spit venom—they spit electric bolts. The marbles crackled, frying some of parts inside, and the sparks clung to the machinery until the wind scraped them off. Now Nox knew why Rassa needed the monowheel to be enclosed.

They continued on, zig-zagging back and forth in the cat-and-mouse chase. They entered a sand tunnel and looped around it as they marbled onwards. They passed through a field of fake cacti with electrified needles, where they were both forced to slow down after one or two accidental jolts. Some systems conked out, which others kicked in from the surge of power. Why, it was just how Porridge liked it.

Then they entered a dug-out maze inside a plateau, where they rolled this way and that, turning here and there, not only trying to find their way through, but find each other. It wasn't so much a cat-and-mouse game then as a game of hide-and-seek. And they were both hiding. And they were both seeking. It wasn't clear at all if they were going in the right direction until they cleared the exit.

When they emerged from these obstacles, they

were back out in an area of pits and pathways, as if they'd made no progress at all. There was an old saying about not being able to see the forest for the trees. Well, when you were down here, you couldn't see the arena for all the obstacles that made it. And with night staring down, you were lucky if you saw anything at all.

They rolled across a convex curve in the desert wall, fighting gravity with the power of their engines. If they didn't keep rolling upwards as well as forwards, they would've tumbled down into the deep ravine below. It didn't matter what you fought gravity with down there.

Then Rassa's marble began to dip, and Nox knew he was having trouble with the engine.

"He's fallin'," the Coilhunter said.

"Oh! Let him!"

"No," Nox said. "He's just another one of the lost." He grabbed the controls for the mechanical arm and swiftly moved it into place. Outside, it grasped the rim of Rassa's vehicle just in time before it slipped over the edge.

"Got 'im."

"Oh, you've got him, alright, peach," Porridge said. "And he's got us!"

The weight of the extra marble was a bit too much. They started to drift towards the edge.

"Nox!" Porridge cried. "I can't stop it!"

"You have to."

"I can't, plum! I can't! Oh!"

Nox stared down at Rassa's marble.

"You've got to drop him!" Porridge said.

Nox didn't reply. He tried to calculate how to drop the marble and then catch it again when Porridge had regained some ground. He tried to tell himself that Rassa was probably bad, that he deserved to die. He tried to see if he could remember the path to the castle if Rassa couldn't lead the way.

Then he tried to hang on for dear life as both marbles tumbled over the edge.

Chapter Twenty-seven

THE ARENA BELOW

The darkness smothered them. The fall felt like forever. Maybe that was how death felt. No one ever came back to tell you. So, maybe you fell. Maybe you kept on falling. Maybe life was like waking from a falling dream.

Then the impact came, and it was surprisingly cushioned. As soon as they struck, they tumbled again, down and around a spiralling slope. All of this was in darkness, but they could feel it, could feel their heads in a spin.

Then it stopped.

Then the lights came on.

There they were, both marbles largely intact, deep underground. The path continued on ahead of them, illuminated by many more lights. Except these weren't oil-lit lanterns like the ones above. These were powered by electricity. It seemed the Man with the Silver Mane wasn't so frugal after all.

The chase continued now in the labyrinth of tunnels, with lights coming on as they approached, and turning off as they left. It was economical, Nox'd give it that. It was the kind of economical you'd attribute to the Dew Distributors or the Treasury, who had a way of making that economy work in their favour. Now the Man with the Silver Mane was doing the same with a new kind of currency: power. Not the power of kings and emperors, but boy could it get you that too.

As they advanced, Nox spotted something on the ground. Rollers. He wondered for a long time what they were for, until it dawned on him. They were another way to generate electricity, using motion. Every time a vessel passed over them, they spun, and the Man with the Silver Mane converted that movement into electricity. He had to. He needed as much power as he could muster. He was using everything—and everyone—to get it.

So, you didn't fall, Rassa, Nox realised. *You led us onto the hamster wheel.*

This truth presented a dilemma: If they stopped the chase, they would stop fuelling the machinery above—and whatever dark aim was meant by it— but they would never find the way into the castle of sand. If they kept going, they would be unwitting accomplices in the Man with the Silver Mane's evil plan. Well, Nox assumed it was evil. It could've been a plan to heal the world, but if you did it with slaves, then, by default, it was evil. Some folk said that about the Wild North as a whole. Well, by default, Nox was a hunter.

So, the hunt continued, because without the hunt, there was no Coilhunter. Some said there was no such thing as settled life in the Wild North, because you were always on the run. You ran from the law, or you *were* the law, and you ran after the wicked. If it weren't for the fierce winds, you'd see a lot of criss-crossing bootprints in the sand.

They tumbled across more rollers, but some of these were armed with spikes, which would've punctured the tyres of the motorbike gangs. Luckily for Rassa, the monowheel had landship treads, which crunched and crushed those spikes, which was lucky for the Dandyman, as there were enough openings for those spikes to pierce through.

They approached a passage that alternated between steps and slopes. If you waited long enough, which wasn't long, you'd see the steps collapse down into a smooth surface. Either was an obstacle, depending on if you were rolling or running. Rassa didn't time his ascent right, so when the steps popped up, they forced him back down, right into the Dandyman, which was knocked back in turn. Then Rassa used the grapnel launchers attached to the monowheel to get him back up again, using the Coilhunter's weapons against him. That hurt Nox's pride, sure enough, but you didn't get to do that long before the Coilhunter hurt you back.

Porridge made the climb up that slope, and it was definitely a climb for the second half, because the steps came out. He had to chug up one step at a time using the propellers for leverage. The Dandyman was a vessel built out of a bit of everything, which made it the right vessel for a bit of everything as well. Stairs or slopes. Sky or sea. It'd keep on rolling.

The walls grew narrower, tearing off a propeller as Porridge slammed into a turn. They were losing Rassa in the labyrinth, and could only follow him by the glimmer of light up ahead, which was quickly fading. If they lost him completely, it was anyone's guess how they'd find their way, or get out at all. Maybe the Man with the Silver Mane would keep them rolling forever, generating energy for him, his own little pet hamsters. It was a defeating thought for Porridge, but for Nox it was an encouraging one. He knew just how well his own pets did.

Chapter Twenty-eight

THE BITS LEFT BEHIND

Bitnickle rolled up to Duck, who just sat there gawking. She turned her radio on, which was her voice, and tuned into various Regime channels.

"We *must* find them," she said, and it was the voice of General Newman of the Regime, speaking about the hunt for Rommond and Taberah of the Resistance. It was part of a regularly scheduled appearance by the general, who had gained an element of celebrity among the Regime.

Duck stared back blankly.

"I have formulated … a plan," Bitnickle said, using snippets from a broadcast from one of the Regime's top munitions experts, discussing new weaponised gases in the works, and back to the same show by the general, who had a new plan of capture every week. It became a running joke among some Resistance fighters, who nicknamed him General New-plan. It wasn't a popular joke though, because too many had faced Newman, and they didn't come away laughing—if they came away at all.

Duck stared back blankly at the clockwork construct.

"Follow me," Bitnickle said, and this time it was a

broadcast from the Iron Emperor himself. The voice was powerful and hypnotic, like the voice of a god. It was no wonder that so many followed him. It was no wonder then that Duck, who continued to stare back blankly, waddled after Bitnickle, as if she were the Coilhunter himself.

The two little mechanical creatures wandered far across the desert, following tracks and signals, until they found Old Reliable on the trail. He looked a little dejected, even a little resigned, but he had some of the Coilhunter's determination in him. He'd smelled Chance Oakley on him, and that'd brought back all those fond memories. He wasn't just going to live. He was going to live up to his name.

Chapter Twenty-nine

A SMALLER KIND OF HUNT

The lights ahead finally faded to nothing, and Nox and Porridge knew Rassa had escaped. The Dandyman rolled on for a moment, following the path of guesswork, which wasn't much of a path at all. Then the Coilhunter commanded Porridge to halt the vehicle.

"The chase is over," he said.

"But I thought you never gave up the hunt, plum."

"I don't." Nox untethered himself and stretched. "Rassa was only important to help us find the door. Well, we've found it. We're *in* the door now. We just need to find a way to open it. The real hunt is for the Man with the Silver Mane."

Even here, Nox could feel the faint presence of that villain. He wasn't sure if he was just imagining it, and it wasn't strong enough to follow. If anything, you'd think twice about following the breadcrumbs left behind by a Magus. You never quite knew where they'd lead.

"Now that we're not rolling," Porridge said, stepping awkwardly over the strewn junk inside his vessel, "I feel a lot less at ease. What if we're stuck here forever, cabbage? Oh! The thought of it!"

"We'd die before forever," Nox said calmly.

"You're not helping, peach."

"Well, *they'll* die before we do."

Nox stepped out of one of the missing windows. Porridge followed, almost slipping on the rollers. He grabbed Nox's arm for support.

"What are we looking for?" Porridge whispered. Nox smiled at the fact that he whispered. They'd more than announced their arrival. The Coilhunter was fine with that. And he was fine with not getting there too quickly either. He wanted to make the bad guys wait. He wanted to make them fester, to stew in the broth of fear. After all, that's what they did for the Wild North.

"A way up," Nox said in time. He inspected the walls, running his gloved fingers through the cracks. This was the kind of villain who had a lair, so Nox wouldn't be surprised to find secret passages. He had some of his own back in his workshop. He didn't like the idea that the good and the bad thought the same.

"Oh! We'll never search all these tunnels!" Porridge exclaimed.

"Not alone," Nox said. He reached for his belt and tossed a box to Porridge with such speed that the trader thought he'd been gunned down. It was lucky it was a box, and he was lucky he was a good guy—of sorts—or the thought might've been more real.

Nox pulled another box from his belt and used both hands to push all four buttons on either side at the same time. It opened, and out fluttered a small mechanical bird. He repeated the same process, while Porridge inspected his box. In time, three little canaries perched on Nox's index finger.

"I used to just bring two of these," he rasped. "But you can bet on finding three passages more often than two. Well, I ain't no bettin' man. I'm a learnin' man."

He hooshed the birds away, and they fluttered off down different tunnels. Nox watched the blinking red dots on his tracker, between glances at the walls, ceiling, and floor.

"But plum! There are more than three passages here."

"Well, let that be my learning-mark for next time, as the tribes say."

"Yes, honey, and the Lost Tribe has their own saying: *to live is to be lost*. And oh! I want to live, strawberry. But not down here. Oh! Not *lost* down here."

Nox spotted one of the dots pulsing erratically. "Well, you don't have to." He led Porridge to where the canary was pecking at a wall. Nox felt around the crevices and spotted a small hole at the bottom, just enough to poke a finger through.

"A wall," Porridge said, rolling his eyes. "Oh! What a find!"

Nox pulled a matchbox from his belt, slid open the cover, and delicately took out the tiny mechanical mouse inside. A mouse with a tiny dark chamber made into its back, allowing it to take black and white photographs. It was novel technology in Altadas, the product of a deal with old Five-pence Tully, who wandered the Wild North with her camera, showing people what they really looked like—for a price. She was an enterprising woman, so she sold her technology to the Coilhunter, and sold him photographs and intel from her travels. Nox was pretty sure she sold the same to the bad guys too.

Nox widened the hole in the wall as much as he could, then let the mechanical mouse scurry through. They waited for a moment, Nox resting against the wall, practising his draw. Porridge pressed his face against the floor and his eye against the opening, but couldn't see much bar a pinprick of light on the other side.

"You're a man of wonders, plum," the trader said, sitting back with a handheld mirror to fix his hair. "How do you have the time for all these toys?"

"How do you have the time for all those clothes?" Nox replied.

"I make the time."

Nox smiled with his eyes. "Well, I do too."

What he didn't say was why. He sectioned off a part of his day for what was once his old job as a toymaker, and now had become a kind of ritual. He used the assembled parts in his workplace, or whatever he could find on his travels, to make a little something. Maybe it couldn't do much. Maybe it was just for show. Maybe it was a reminder of the way things used to be, when he made toys for his kids, and toys for other kids too. Far too often it became something else. An idea, sparked by his hidden fuel of rage, turned those cute little creatures into something more. There was a time when being a plaything was enough. Now they had to be more. Now they had to be useful. Now they were just another soldier in the war.

They heard a squeak, and the mouse returned. Nox placed it back in the matchbox, which was more than it seemed, and waited for the film to develop. In time, he had several one-inch photographs, which he inspected with an eyeglass. Some of them were too blurry or too dark to show much, but one was clear enough. There was a giant wheel on the other side, leading to a hatch in the ceiling.

"Well, now," Nox said. "We've found our way up."

He couldn't help but add a little something in his thoughts: *The real hamster wheel.*

Chapter Thirty

THE WRECKING BALL

There was a way out, sure enough, but there wasn't yet a way to get there. Sometimes when you were in the maze, you saw the centre through the hedges, but no matter how close you were, you knew you'd have to go farther away to find it. Often that was when you knew you were truly lost.

But the Coilhunter was the lawmaker, and that meant he made his own rules. If you were one hedge away from the centre, then you trimmed that hedge. If you were one wall away, then you knocked down that wall. Some said that made him just as bad as the lawbreakers, but folk tended not to say that around him.

"How do we get through?" Porridge asked. "Oh! Don't take me for a mouse, dearie!"

Not a mouse, no, but he sure did squeak like one. It was lucky that this was not a mission of stealth, even though it probably should've been, or Porridge's high-pitched squeals would've echoed up to the Man with the Silver Mane. No. He *knew* they were coming. It made Nox second guess his plan. Most villains didn't invite him back for a visit.

"Do you have explosives?" Nox asked, pointing

back to the Dandyman, which typically had a bit of everything in its holds, or netted to the walls, or nailed to the ceiling.

"I *had*," Porridge said with a pout, "but I cast my dynamite out before we started this game of marbles. Oh, I didn't want us blowing up! Oh! The thought! And oh! The irony that we'd need it now, sugar. One gorgeous, leather boot forward, two steps backward! Oh!"

Nox wasn't entirely surprised, though often he was more surprised at what he *did* find in Porridge's eccentric vessel. Some called Nox the Guru of Gadgets, but Porridge was the Guru of Oddballs and Oddthings. Sometimes you'd find not quite what you wanted, but what you *needed* there.

"Don't you have any of your own?" Porridge enquired.

"No," Nox said. He wasn't the type for fireworks, though he'd developed some small explosive devices in his workshop. He knew well the power of it, having fought TNT Tom, and having pulled down posters for Soasa Sanders, the so-called Dynamite Lady of the Resistance. Few exceeded her skill with explosives, and the Regime had lost many important crossings to her handiwork.

"Oh!" Porridge cried, with the back of his hand against his forehead. "We're forsaken!"

Nox was silent for a moment. "How durable is the Dandyman?"

"What's that, plum? *Durable*? Oh, why it's a veritable fortress!"

"Good, because—"

"As long as you don't bash it against something."

"Ah."

Porridge toyed with his mouth. "I'm assuming that's the plan then."

"Unless we can think of a better one."

"Oh, my spinning cogs! My mind is frazzled, dearie. Look to me for something pretty, not for *ideas*! Oh!"

"Well, then, let's get this ball movin' again."

"But there's no space here to get a proper run-up, sweetie. How will we create enough force to break the wall?"

"We'll use it like a wreckin' ball." Nox said.

"Oh! But how, plum?"

"The arm. It'll give us leverage."

Porridge was about to object again, but Nox silenced him with a puff of black smoke from his mask. "Trust me," he rasped. And boy did you trust him when he told you with gravel, because you never wanted him to tell you with a pistol. They say you should listen to a man with a voice of grit, or you might find yourself breathing gravel of a different kind. They do say a lot, don't they?

Porridge brought the Dandyman down the tunnel, and Nox set up the mechanical arm so that it burrowed into the ceiling and grasped on there like a grappling hook. Inside, the Coilhunter manned the controls, while Porridge fainted at the sight of his poor vessel being abused in such a manner. The ball swung back, then forward, bashing into the wall. It lost a propeller on the first impact, but it lost those plenty on its travels. Again it bashed, and again, until the bricks tumbled. Soon enough, the makeshift wrecking ball had revealed a way into the large chamber that housed the hamster wheel.

"Oh! A bit of luck at last!" Porridge cried.

It was then that they heard the sound of a grate opening. Light streamed into the chamber, illuminating the silhouettes of many collared wolves. It seemed they were like the Coilhunter. They didn't give up the chase.

Chapter Thirty-one

THE HAMSTER WHEEL

The wolves looked towards them, and Nox looked towards the towering wooden wheel, rotating slowly. He gauged the distance to it, and the distance to the wolves, and thought the latter a little shorter. But he wasn't going to run to them. He wasn't going to fight them and kill them again, if they were even the same wolves as before.

"Quick!" Nox shouted, grabbing Porridge by the arm. He ran, and he pulled the scavenger with him. They dashed towards the wheel, and the wolves darted towards them. Porridge's heels echoed in the chamber, and his yelps and cries punctuated the percussion. It was the music of terror. It was a music well known in the Wild North.

The game of who would get there first played out in almost time-slowed seconds. You could count them clear, maybe because they might be the last ones you got. They say Death comes swift and sudden in the Wild North, but Death is no gunslinger. He'll drag out your final moments by making the seconds count down all the slower. He'll give you just long enough to see him, to feel the terror before the blackness. Well now, that's what folk said about the Coilhunter too.

Two wolves advanced ahead of the pack, their legs vanishing into a blur. Their mouths became wider. Their snarls became louder. Nox and Porridge could see now that they weren't quite running *away* from those beasts, but *towards* them, to that point of union in the middle, that big old creaking wheel. Folk said things about wheels too. Grim things. Like how more often than not the wheel of life'd roll right over you.

But not if you were inside the wheel.

Just as the wolves came within biting distance, Nox grabbed a hold of Porridge's arm, then punched his left arm forward, launching the grapnel up towards the wheel. It caught in the spokes and tugged them up and out of the gaping maws of the beasts below. The wolves leaped, snapping at Nox's buckled boots.

"Oh!" Porridge cried, trying desperately to get a good hold of Nox's sleeve. They hadn't had time to grasp each other's hands. They hadn't had time to brace their muscles for the pull of gravity, that tug-of-war they knew they couldn't win.

They dangled there, swaying above the waiting wolves, some of which continued to leap up and bite at the air between them. Others scratched and pawed at the wheel. It continued its slow rotation, bringing Nox and Porridge higher, but the higher it went, the more gravity tugged back.

"Oh, don't drop me, berry!" Porridge cried, alternating between looking up at Nox and down at the wolves. "Oh! I'm not made for this! I'm not meant for dog food! Oh!"

The moment caused his scarf to unfurl, revealing his collar. He scrambled with one arm to catch it, but the scarf fluttered down delicately, waving in the air like a flag of peace. The movement was so at odds with the one that followed. The wolves pounced on it and shredded it to pieces.

It was then, as Nox felt Porridge slip a little more, that the Coilhunter saw another image that Death put in his head. He saw the colourful trader plummeting down and being torn apart by the mob of brown and black below. He saw all the vibrant, mismatching colours turn to red. He saw it all play out in those same time-slowed seconds, until he was forced to look away.

Who then would call him plum? Who then would call him peach? Some said the Dandyman could travel to any place, but could it travel to the afterlife? Would it be Porridge's copper-plated coffin? Would it take him to places where he would find other lost souls? Would it take him to the true Lostlands, where neither Death nor Life could wander?

All of these thoughts played out in those harrowing moments, just like they played out for the Coilhunter in his dreadful memories of his family's murder. Just like they played out in his sleep. The nightmares overran him and shoved out the dreams, just like Death had shoved out his family. Folk said Death didn't have a face, but that didn't stop Nox from making a Wanted poster all the same. *Dead or Alive* was moot then. *Double Dead* wasn't.

But Death hadn't yet claimed Porridge. Nox hoped the image wasn't a premonition. He promised himself it wouldn't be. He hated making promises he wasn't sure he could keep.

"Oh!" Porridge cried as he slipped further. Nox's leather gloves were good for many things, but they didn't give him the grip he needed here.

"Oh, Nox!" Porridge fell another inch. The trader called him by his real name. Not *plum*. Not *cabbage*. This was no time for endearment. It was time for desperation.

Porridge's arm slid gradually through the Coilhunter's grasp. There wasn't much Nox could do but wait. One arm was pulled up by the grapnel, the other down by Porridge. He was like a scarecrow, waiting for the crows to peck.

Their hands came close together now, and it was time to grasp the other. It had to be perfectly timed, because Death was a perfectionist. They say the Devil's in the details. Well, if you look closely, you'll see Death there as well. The careless and the clumsy were gunned down long before anyone else, long before the watchful and the prepared. But long or short, Death got you all the same. He didn't just wait for the perfect moments. He made them.

Now was one of them.

Gravity yanked all the harder. The wolves salivated below.

The moment came when Porridge slipped several inches, and their fingers grazed each other. They clung on, forming a tenuous grasp. Already, even with the renewed vigour of their interlocked hands, they could feel the slipping continue. There were no other hands to grasp now. Just the hand of God. And there was one thing you learned quick in the Wild North. God would let you fall.

"Don't let me go, Nox!"

Nox breathed out an exasperated plume of smoke. He didn't say anything. He didn't make a further promise. He didn't tell Porridge he would hold on forever. He didn't waste his energy with words when the veins and sinews in his arms bulged.

Then Nox felt his glove edging down his fingers. His own sweat betrayed him and nudged the glove down a little further. It didn't entirely matter how tightly Porridge clung. He would fall with glove in hand. That fashionless, brown glove. They say there was no accounting for taste. Well, tell that to the salivating wolves.

Porridge glanced up at Nox, but now he didn't say anything either. He could feel the shifting glove. He could feel his own body shifting too. The hamster wheel brought them higher, high enough to make the fall deeper. That was how Death did it in the Wild North. He let you escape the gunslinger's bullet, only to die to the scorpion's sting.

Porridge took a deep breath. His eyes watered. "Keep on drifting," he whispered, in case Death overheard. But Death heard everything.

Nox didn't have time to shout "No!" He didn't have time to make a last ditch effort to grasp at nothing. All he had time for was what Death allowed in the time-slowed seconds. Time enough to see Porridge fall.

Chapter Thirty-two

THE WHEEL OF LIFE
AND DEATH

Porridge tumbled. It was fitting, perhaps, because that's how he went through life in the Dandyman. Folk said there wasn't much you could do about death, but you could go out in a fitting manner. That was how you made your death honour your life. Well, the robbers often went out robbing. The gunmen often went out gunning. Few would say there was any honour in that.

But Nox had dug too many graves. He wasn't digging another one for Porridge.

He fired the grapnel from his right arm down, letting the wire wrap around Porridge's foot before the hook latched into place. It was a move he'd practised a thousand times before, but it never removed that little moment of doubt, that little worry that the hook wouldn't live up to its name.

Porridge screamed as he swooped above the head of the wolves. They jumped, coming mere inches from his face. One of them landed with a golden-brown curl in its fangs.

"Pull me up! Pull me up! Oh! I'm no pendulum!"

Nox grunted from the strain. "Oh, you're gonna

have to be."

Nox swung Porridge from side to side, gaining speed and distance with each swing. Higher now. Faster. Porridge shrieked as he swung out of the gnashing teeth of the wolves, and then shrieked all the louder as he steered back into them. The wolves paced back and forth with every swing. Then, with a final effort, Nox swung him up to one of the spokes of the wheel, where Porridge grasped on tight.

"Take it off your leg!" Nox shouted.

"Oh, I can't, pumpkin! I'll fall! Oh!"

"Take it off! Now!"

What Porridge didn't realise was that the part of the wheel Nox's first grapnel hooked onto had reached the top and was now starting to go down again. They thought they'd dangled close to the wolves before, but they could always dangle closer.

"We're goin' down!" Nox yelled.

That was enough to motivate Porridge, as was the tug of the wire on his leg. He reached with one hand to free it, but the wire pulled his leg up more, until it was horizontal. Then it pulled further, until he was horizontal too, clinging onto the spoke with all his might.

"Oh! Oh! Help! Help!"

Nox manoeuvred himself so that he could stretch down towards his arm and unstrap the grapnel launcher with his teeth. It flung away, until it snapped against Porridge's leg. The scavenger almost toppled from his position.

"Use it to get up here," Nox shouted down. He was already climbing the wheel, using the other grappling hook to pull him up.

Porridge strapped the grapnel launcher onto his arm, finding it wasn't a good fit, and certainly wasn't fashionable. He was tempted to grasp the wire for extra surety, but decided against it when an image of his rope-burned hands came into his head. He aimed, clung onto the launcher with his other hand, and fired. The hook blasted into thin air, then came hurtling back down, past the shrieking Porridge, and knocked out one of the wolves below. The other wolves backed away from this new metal predator.

"Again!" Nox shouted. He was almost at the top of the wheel now. Folk said the top was a precarious location, because it seemed like the best place to be. But the wheel was always turning, which meant it'd be the bottom soon enough. So, the wise would say that maybe when you were on top, you shouldn't go sneering at the folk below.

Porridge bashed the buttons on the launcher, triggering the recoil. The hook latched back into place and he tried again. This time he hit the mark, and the hook hauled him up, kicking and screaming, towards one of the higher spokes. From there, he was just a helping hand away from Nox's position. The Coilhunter might've had a spare set of gloves, but he offered his bare hand this time.

"Don't drop me again," Porridge urged.

Nox pulled him up, and both of them straddled the top of the wheel, walking in place against its rotations.

"Remind me to leave the adventures to you, peach," Porridge said. "Oh! I'm all but done for!"

"You're not done yet," Nox said. He took back the grapnel from Porridge and fastened it on his arm. Then he grabbed Porridge by the waist, fired upwards, and let the wire haul them up into the open hatch. They climbed up, leaving the wolves pacing and howling below.

"Now," Nox said, striking a match. It illuminated a small room with granite walls. It could've been anywhere, but Nox could already feel that presence a little stronger. They were out of the cellars and into the main levels now.

The castle of sand, Nox thought. He couldn't help but think of the sand castles the children made. *His* children made. There were few oceans to wash them away, but most crumbled to the wind and the sandstorms, or to landship treads, or to thick, leather boots. He thought this abode of the Man with the Silver Mane would have to fall to his own.

Chapter Thirty-three

THE BACK DOOR GUARD

With many lairs, you could expect less resistance if you went in the back door. This was some lair though, and Nox expected little resistance at all. After all, the Man with the Silver Mane wanted him to return. It'd all but suit to leave the back door open.

And it *was* open.

The light streamed in from the other room, where three figures huddled around a table, playing cards. They had stacks of coils to their names. They didn't bet in halves and quarters. Nox was familiar with that. And their names? Well, Nox was familiar with those too.

There was Hammerback Harry, who, unsurprisingly, had a big old two-handed hammer strapped to his back. In the olden days, folk said there was only honour in sword and shield. In the days of the gunslinger, folk said there was only honour in the fastest draw. Well, Hammerback Harry had no time for honour. He smashed it with his hammer like he smashed the skulls of folk who said too much.

Then there was Rustbucket Riley, who wore a helmet made from an old mop bucket. He claimed to be descended from an old family of knights, and this was his way of paying homage to his ancestors. He could talk for hours about heraldry and chivalry. He even had a sword. But when it came down to it, he fought with a pistol all the same.

And there was Buckhorn Bobby, also known as Boomin' Bray, because he had a voice like thunder. Folk said you couldn't help but fall for him if you heard him holler, and some said women queued up by the dozen to hear him say their name. What wasn't just rumour though was that he could tell a mean old tale. And boy did he tell them. It seemed like he had a new one every day.

Together, this trio made up the Back Door Guard, an oddball bunch hired by the Man with the Silver Mane to guard the underground entrance to his fortress. They were among the lost too, sure enough, but the difference was they didn't want to be found. They had a chequered past, like most in the Wild North, but they wanted to keep it chequered, not change it all to black or white. They weren't a bad bunch, as far as the Wild North went, but they had a habit of being hired by the bad. They were happy to hide away here in the dark cellars, chugging down beer, sharing stories, and staying out of the spotlight.

Well, Nox wasn't just the law. He was, as some folk dubbed him, the Man Who Shines in the Shadows. When you faced him, you knew damn well you were going to be dragged into the light.

"What's that?" Rustbucket Riley said, shifting suddenly in his seat.

"Probably just that tin head o' yours," Hammerback Harry said.

"Surprised he can hear anything rollin' 'round in there at all!" Buckhorn Bobby hollered, and he let out a boisterous laugh.

"I'm tellin' ya, I heard somethin'."

Hammerback Harry plucked an eyebrow and stared at it. "You're always hearin' things."

They didn't notice Nox in the shadows of the doorway, guitar in hand. He played his signature tune, which some played in taverns across the Wild North, singing bone-rattling songs of the Man with a Thousand Names. The music had a sinister twang. It told you the Coilhunter was coming. It told you he was coming for you.

The Back Door Guard almost toppled from their chairs. Cards went flying, but just as quick came the weapons. Hammerback Harry heaved his heavy hammer into hand. Rustbucket Riley had one hand on his sheathed sword, but the other on his drawn pistol. Buckhorn Bobby had his rifle out, replete with an iron sight for accuracy. You might've heard him coming, but the bullets would come first.

Smoke billowed into the room, pouring out of Nox's guitar. He vanished into the haze, casting two noisemakers in either direction. They mimicked the sound of his boots. But the Back Door Guard knew that. They'd encountered him before. That's why they hid out here in the Lostlands, hoping they'd never encounter him again. They turned in every direction, standing now back to back, pointing their weapons east and west, and north and south. They didn't swing wildly or waste bullets at phantom sounds or spectral sights. They knew Nox was patient. They knew they'd have to be patient too.

"Come out, you Gosh-darn Masked Menace!" Buckhorn Bobby shouted. The sound rattled off the walls, drowning out the noisemakers. Dust crumbled from the cracks in the ceiling.

Rustbucket Riley put a hand on Bobby's shoulder. He gestured with his head towards the door. He heard another sound there. The sound of someone approaching.

They turned to the door, weapons at the ready. The footsteps came closer. That's how they knew it wasn't a noisemaker, unless Nox was still out there, rolling one of those distractions their way. Hammerback Harry patted his hand with his hammer. Rustbucket Riley pointed his shuddering pistol. Buckhorn Bobby squinted into the sight on his rifle.

Then *he* emerged from the doorway. First he was just a silhouette, but he didn't quite seem as intimidating as they remembered. Then, as the light hit and penetrated through the smoke, they saw him in all his terrible glory.

Well, what a sight he was.

"Oh!" Porridge exclaimed, putting both hands to his lips. "Were you expecting someone else, honeybushes?"

The Back Door Guard blinked, incredulous. Then Nox's hands emerged from the smoke behind them, seizing Rustbucket Riley by the helmet. He quickly swivelled it around, until the eye sockets faced the wrong way, then wrapped his unstrapped grapnel launcher around the handle of Hammerback Harry's weapon. Just as they turned to fight, he fired the hook upwards, letting it grasp the chandelier. Harry never did let go of that hammer easy, so he went upwards with the recoil, his feet dangling over the bumbling of his fellows below.

"You!" Buckhorn Bobby roared. Nox was too close for him to use his sight, but a round of gunfire sent the Coilhunter back into the haze. Bobby turned swiftly back to Porridge, but couldn't find him at the door.

"Take that off, you fool!" Bobby told Rustbucket Riley, who hadn't quite turned his helmet back into place. It was lucky, though, that he didn't, because Hammerback Harry had just unstrapped the grapnel launcher, and he fell, hammer in hand, right on top of Riley. The hammer clobbered him in the head, knocking him out cold.

"Play fair," Harry said, swiping at the shadows. "Or don't play at all!"

The duo turned this way and that, stumbling over the body of dozing Riley, who might've been glad to be out of the game. Some said it was better to lose quick than think you ever had a chance of winning. That was a motto of sorts for the Wild North. Many, willingly or not, lived by it. But then, they died by it too.

"You're in for a surprise, Coilhunter!" Buckhorn Bobby brayed. "Wait 'til you meet the man upstairs!"

The last of the smoke cleared, and they turned to find Nox seated at the table, cards in one hand, pistol in the other, and a look on his face like he had a winning hand. "I've already met 'im," he rasped. "How's about I send you to meet the *real* man upstairs?"

Hammerback Harry came lunging, smashing down on the table, breaking it in two. Nox was already in the air, aided by his other grappling hook. Buckhorn Bobby aimed, but Nox's pinpoint gunfire took out Bobby's sight. Nox didn't need an augment on his weapon for that.

Bobby roared, and the room shook. "I'll shoot you blind then!"

Bullets pinged off the ceiling and the walls, but Nox was back down on the floor again. He tripped up Bobby, yanked the rifle from his hands, then turned and fired. Hammerback Harry's hoisted hammer slipped out of his own blasted hands. He yelped as he looked at his skint fingers.

"Now," Nox said, casting a rope from his belt towards Harry. "Why don't you go and tie yourselves up while there's still parts to tie."

Bobby sauntered over to Harry reluctantly. "We coulda taken ya."

Nox smiled. "Sure," he said. He nodded towards Rustbucket Riley on the floor. "Why, he's takin' me right now."

Harry tied up Bobby and Riley, then let Nox do the same for him. Without their weapons, they weren't much of a guard. They at least had enough grazes and bruises to show the Man with the Silver Mane that they'd tried. They had a deep, unsettling feeling that they'd need to find new work soon enough.

With the trio tied up, and their weapons on the other side of the room, Porridge strolled through and gave a finger wave. "Toodles," he said. "And no hard feelings. Oh!"

Nox opened the door to the hallway leading to the prison cells of the castle of sand.

"Don't think I don't know your names," Nox rasped. "I'm just waitin' for the posters now."

"Go ahead an' wait then!" Buckhorn Bobby boomed.

Nox looked back with fire in his eyes. "Somethin' tells me I won't be waitin' long."

Chapter Thirty-four

THE CELLAR

With Buckhorn Bobby's earthquake echoes fading behind them, Nox and Porridge found themselves approaching a seemingly endless row of jail cells. The first several dozen of these were empty, though there were signs of struggle at some. The farther they went, however, the more prisoners they found, wearing those same collars that united them all.

"Are you here to free us?" an old man said, reaching a bony arm out for them.

"Yes," Nox said, "and jail your captor."

"Don't!" a woman cried from several cells down. "Don't let us out!"

Porridge frolicked up to her. "Why not? Oh! You poor thing!"

"That's what he wants."

"Surely he wants you prisoner," Nox said.

The woman reefed her fingers through her hair. "We'll do things to you."

Porridge backed away.

"We won't want to," she continued. "But we will."

"Don't listen to her," the old man shouted, his voice hoarse. "Help us!"

"We'll fight you," the woman said. "He'll make us fight. He *wants* us to fight."

"Maybe, you know, we'll come back," Porridge suggested. "Right, plum?"

"Sure," Nox said, but he didn't make it a promise. While he had that collar on, he felt he'd only be back if the Man with the Silver Mane wanted him to go back.

"Fools!" the old man shouted after them as they continued on. "Cowards and fools!"

"You're no better than him!" another cried out.

"You're no better than us!" a third added.

They continued on, passing cell after cell. Some spoke. Some reached out. Many others curled up and did nothing but wait. They'd already made their fight. There was nothing left. No energy. No fuel. No will. It was a sorry sight to see so many people like this. It took a lot not to try to free them immediately.

"Oh, my ripened raspberries!" Porridge said. "This *is* a depressing place! Oh! What if they could help us?"

"I think most of them can't help themselves," Nox replied. "Many of them were helpless before they came out here. They were already broken. They were already lost."

"Lord, now there's a sight for sore eyes," a familiar voice said.

They halted and turned towards the nearest cell. It wasn't just a familiar voice. It was a familiar body. Broad shoulders, a little stocky, with a craggy face and a head of white hair. A little overgrown, maybe, and a bushy white moustache to match. Then there were the eyes, brown and deep. He wasn't just a man of years. He was a man who'd seen a lot happen over those years.

It was Chance Oakley.

Chapter Thirty-five

FOUND

Nox didn't think twice about letting Oakley out. He wasn't like the others. The Coilhunter *knew* him, and knew that no matter what the Man with the Silver Mane did to him, he was a good man, who'd only ever do good things—even if it was against his own interests. They'd met when Nox was on the run from the other bounty hunters of the Wild North, after he'd been framed for the massacre of a tribal village. Unlike many, Oakley had given him a chance to prove himself. That was how he got his name. Chance Oakley always gave folk second chances.

"Oh! We found you! Oh!" Porridge shouted with glee. He did a little dance on the spot, which must've looked odd to the other prisoners—if they weren't so used to seeing unusual things.

"An' about damn time," Oakley said.

Nox took a lockpick kit from his belt and made short work of the prison door. It slid open with a creak.

"Are you injured?" Nox asked, helping the drifter to his feet.

Oakley dusted off his hat and put it on. "Just my soul. Ain't nothin' you can do 'bout that."

"I wasn't sure we'd find you," the Coilhunter admitted.

"Oh, *I* was, Nathaniel. I was. That's about all I was sure of. Lord, I made a right ol' mess of things venturin' out here. Didn't make it three days 'fore I was attacked by wolves. Barely got my rescue signal off or maybe you wouldn't have known at all. Too bad it attracted the Lost Tribe too."

"Why did you come out here, Chance?" Nox asked. "What were you hopin' to find?"

"You know, I've asked myself that several times now," Oakley said, ruffling his moustache. "I've been a drifter for a long time now, lookin' for answers here and there. Sometimes I thought I found 'em, and then the answers seemed to sieve through my hands like sand. So I kept on lookin'. I went to the tribes. I went to the gangs. Lord, I went to the cults and the priests too. All of 'em had a version to tell me. All of 'em had a spin on the truth. Not the full truth, mind, just a taster. Quite a lot of truths. Quite a lot of journeys. And shucks, I still felt lost."

"But here," Nox said. "There ain't anything to find out here."

Oakley chuckled. "Is that so, huh? Well, bet you ain't never thought you'd find a fortress out here. Well, truth is I was at breakin' point, so I came out here in desperation. You see, when my wife and friends abandoned me after my gold mine collapsed, I lost all hope. Lord, I hate to say it, but I lost the will to live. I was just gettin' by, day by day. When I came out of my slump, I started my journey, and I thought I got enough answers to keep me goin'. I told myself I was over it, Nox, but I'm not. I just learned to hide the part of me that hurts."

"We all do," Nox said. "It's how we survive."

"But I want to do more than just survive. I want to live. I want to thrive."

"Oh, don't we all, hun," Porridge said.

"So, in a moment of bleakness," Oakley continued, "in a time of uncertainty, I decided to come out here. It was one of the few places drifters like me go for answers, mind, and I hadn't gone yet. So, I thought I'd either find my answers out here or—Lord, forgive me for sayin' it—I'd find my grave."

"Well, you almost did," Nox said.

"My grave, yes. Still lookin' for those answers."

"I ain't no philosopher," the Coilhunter rasped, "but did ya not ever think that maybe you were lookin' in the wrong place? Folk go from town to town, from teachin' to teachin', always lookin' outside themselves. Did ya not ever think to look within?"

That was how Nox found his own answers, how he found his mission, his purpose. Oh, he looked outwards at first, at the lawlessness of the Wild North. But then he looked inside and found that he could do something about it, that he could be his own kind of sheriff. There was no one to give him the badge. Not even God. He had to make it and pin it on himself.

"You know, Nathaniel, I did," Oakley said with a sigh, "but I guess I was afraid o' what I'd find. I always thought of myself as a strong man. But what if I'm not so strong? What if, without the ol' missus and my ol' chums, I'm not all I was cracked up to be?"

"Then you start a new you. If your old life was

built on them, you build a new one."

"I guess I'm just afraid to let 'em go."

"What is there to let go? They're gone. They didn't really love you or they'd still be here. They wouldn't have jumped ship after the Regime came, just 'cause gold was no longer valuable. They would've stuck it out, rich or poor."

"See, I get that," Oakley said. "Logically, that all adds up. Lord, I ain't anyone to argue against logic. But you see, none of that changes how I feel. It's these Gosh-darn emotions that're eatin' me up. They contradict the logic, and I have good days where I'm thinkin' straight, and bad days where it's all heart and no head. That's how I ended up out here. Lord, no head at all!"

"Oh, dearie, I wouldn't be so hard on the heart," Porridge said. "It sometimes leads to good places the head will never go. Oh!"

"True enough there," Oakley said, tipping his hat to Porridge. "True enough."

"I'm Porridge, by the way." Porridge extended his hand, more to kiss it than shake it.

"G'day, Porridge, an' fair greetings to ya." Oakley didn't give Porridge the usual look most did on first meeting him. He didn't bat an eye at this attire. He didn't judge his posture. He made no internal comments about his voice. By Oakley's ethos, you didn't ever judge a man. It didn't matter what they wore, how they got there, or even what they'd done. Everyone deserved a chance. The Wild North wasn't going to give it to you. Most folk wouldn't either. By Oakley's reckoning, it was no wonder so many were bad. They'd never been given a chance to be good.

"Now," Nox said. "We've gotta think about how to get you out. And all of these other slaves. We'll have to find a way to remove these collars."

"Some rescue party we were! Oh!" Porridge said.

"From what I've gathered," Oakley said, "that Magus up there's working on some machine. He keeps talkin' about other worlds. Shucks, I've smoked some leaf in my time, and I got a glimpse of 'em, mind, but never did quite believe it after. If I were a different man, I'd wager he was still smokin'! But then who am I to judge? You say you ain't no philosopher. Well, I ain't no magician, and I ain't no scientist. Who's to tell what's really out there?"

"Like the Iron Empire," Porridge pointed out.

"We need to stop him," Nox said. "Whatever he's doin', he's doin' it wrong. He's using folk like fuel. God only knows what he's up to."

And God might've known alright, but he wasn't doing anything about it. You see, in the Wild North, God wore a slave collar too.

Chapter Thirty-six

THE LONG LADDER

Oakley might've been a victim like the rest of them, but he didn't act like it. He hadn't quite found what he was looking for, and wasn't entirely sure he knew what he was looking for in the first place. But he'd found something else. He'd found the Man with the Silver Mane. Sometimes you don't quite drift from place to place, but from mission to mission. That was how the Coilhunter did it. And Oakley'd led him to his latest hunt.

"Up here," Oakley said, leading them to a vent. "These all lead into a larger ventin' chamber, which runs up the centre of the tower. It needs it with all that power generated. It'll be warm, mind. Lord, there'll be steam shootin' outta some of 'em."

"Oh! That sounds terrible! Is there no other way, cabbage?" Porridge asked.

"Well, not without fighting through endless waves of guards."

"That hasn't stopped Nox before, plum."

And that was true, but this time Nox objected. "Let's take the quiet route for now."

Oakley grumbled. "Somethin' tells me he'll still know you're comin.'"

"I'm countin' on it," Nox said. "Let's hope he feels the dread."

They climbed into the vent, which was just big enough to shimmy through on their elbows. Oakley went first, then Nox, with Porridge following reluctantly.

"This'll crumple my clothes!" Porridge complained. "Oh, the things I do for the world! Oh!"

Oakley led them through the maze of vents, left and right, around sharp bends, and seemingly back in a circle, until he pushed through to a colossal venting chamber. They scrambled out and surveyed the area. It was a circular room, which seemed like it went up for miles. They couldn't see the top, but they could see several ladders running up the sides, and many openings spewing out steam along the way.

"Looks like a long climb," Nox said.

Oakley took off his hat and fanned his face. "Well, it's either that or go the long way 'round."

"You know what they say about short cuts, peach," Porridge said.

Oakley put a hand on his shoulder. "Oh, they weren't talkin' 'bout in here."

Nox put a gloved hand on the ladder and shook it. It rattled. "That's not a good sign. Test the other ones."

They did, until Oakley found about the best of the bunch. "Seems as sturdy as we're gonna get."

"We should use different ladders," Nox said. "Just in case."

"In case of what?" Porridge howled. "Oh! I feel like I'm falling already! Oh!"

"The problem is," Oakley said, "we won't all come out at the same place on top."

"We'll have to regroup up there," Nox said. "Let's use the three closest ladders."

"Not the sturdiest?"

"The three closest, *sturdiest* ladders."

Porridge struck a dramatic pose. "Oh! It's like lookin' for coils in the desert!"

"Well," Oakley said with a wry smile, "he *is* the Coilhunter."

They searched again until they found three reasonably sturdy ladders close together. It wasn't an easy search, because just when they found two, the others on either side seemed weak. In the end, they had to opt for two beside each other, and a third that was one ladder away.

They started the climb. Nox took the centre, in case anything happened, and Oakley took the farthest away, because he said he knew this place better than the others—though Nox was sure the drifter didn't know it well enough. If there was one thing you could count on with a Magus, it was that they'd built deception into the walls.

The first few dozen rungs went by swiftly, though Porridge took them slower, as he was still wearing high-heeled boots. Then they came to the first vents. They weren't just on either side, but behind the ladders as well. The trio had to wait and time the blasts of steam, then quickly scramble up during the brief pauses. At first these happened simultaneously, so that all three could time their ascent together. But then they alternated, so one had to wait while another raced up. That made it all the more dangerous, because there was an instinctive urge to climb when others climbed, or wait when others waited. Humans had the instinctive urge to be part of the herd.

Well, that trio might've started as a herd, but they were quickly separated. Not only were they at different heights, but they faced different challenges now.

Nox's ladder was stable, but the vents started to come in pairs now. First they fired together, and he had to scramble all the faster, but then they fired at different times, so that he had to linger over the first one before he could pass the second. Then they came in threes and fours, alternating their scalding puffs. Nox couldn't help but blast out a few puffs from his own vent in exasperation.

All the while, the ladder was getting hotter. Nox could already feel it farther down. He could already feel it through his gloves. He was just glad he had gloves in the first place. Right now, he wished he had spares to give to the others. But even if he did, there was no time for that now. There was barely enough time to climb.

As the heat increased, so too did the frequency of those blasts of steam, which in turn added to the broil. It mounted, degree by degree, until Nox had to grunt in his mask, until he could start to feel his gloves and boots melt a little and stick to the bars. There was no time now to wait for the vents to blast empty. Sometimes you just had to pull the trigger.

So Nox did just that.

He fired his grappling hook up, pulled his hat

down over face, wrapped his coat tight around him, and zipped upwards. He growled as he passed through patches of steam, turning where he could to let it scald the already burnt patches of skin on the back of his head. The fire'd done that to him many years ago. The sun'd added its own crisp after. Now it was the steam's turn to burn.

He barely reached the place the grapnel hooked onto before he fired the second one. He glided up again, through the periodic blasts of steam, until he arrived at the top. He was a little scalded, but there was one good thing about the concoction of chemicals in the tank on his back. It wasn't just oxygen. It didn't just help him breathe. It helped with the pain.

Oakley's ladder was stable, and he faced far fewer vents. For once, the climb was relatively easy. Oh, he was tired, sure, but he was used to that. He was used to the long days of travel, and the short nights of rest. He was used to the road and the journey. Most times you travelled sideways. Sometimes, rarely, you travelled up. And other times, far too often, you travelled down. That was the pervading direction in the Wild North. Folk didn't need to signpost it. Sooner or later, you were going down. Best keep climbing then.

Porridge's ladder seemed stable at first, just enough to get him higher. Then it started to shake. Now, they all shook a little, especially when the steam blasts came. But this one shook a lot. He could hear the rattle. He could *feel* the rattle. Hell, he could see the bolts coming loose.

"Oh!" he cried, wishing he was ascending in the

Dandyman instead of climbing on foot. He wasn't cut out for this, he knew, and yet he found himself being increasingly dragged into the affairs of the Coilhunter, not to mention the war down South. The truth of it, and he'd never admit this, was that he liked the attention. He liked having a place in the big events of the time. He liked knowing that he was doing some good, even if he was doing it in his own oddball way.

But what good could he do if he fell?

"One step at a time," he told himself, but he didn't follow that advice. He tried to take two rungs now. He wasn't sure if that was helping or hindering. Sometimes the faster you went, the slower you got there. And often times the higher you went, the farther you fell. He wondered if maybe he should've been climbing down instead of up. No. He was more than halfway there, or so it seemed in the endless venting chamber. The only way was up.

But a bolt popped loose and pinged off the ladder as it tumbled down below. Porridge didn't even hear its final clink. He couldn't see where it landed. The only way to see it now was to join it. But no. The only way was up.

There were things folk in the Wild North said to themselves every day. Words of wisdom. Promises, even. Like the only way was up. But you see, the Wild North made its own promises. It had its own kind of desert wisdom. It wouldn't just tell you. It'd teach you. The only way is down.

The other bolts came loose, and the ladder bent in half. Porridge clung from it and dangled over the massive drop. He could already feel his grasp weakening. He'd lost a lot of his strength already. You didn't come to the Lostlands to find that.

"Help!" he screamed.

"Hang on!" Nox shouted.

Porridge watched the small figure of the Coilhunter vanish into the doorway. No doubt he was trying to find a way around. No doubt about that at all. What Porridge doubted was whether he'd still be clinging on when Nox got there.

Oakley stood at his own doorway, feeling a little helpless. He knew there wasn't a whole lot a drifter like him could do. He didn't have the Coilhunter's gadgets. He didn't have his survival skills. And he sure as hell didn't have his daring.

Then he turned, and he saw something move in the shadows of the corridor. Something big. Something menacing.

"Careful, now," he told himself, as he reached for the rifle on his back. The Man with the Silver Mane hadn't taken that either. "Careful."

No, he didn't have Nox's gadgets, or skills, or daring. But he knew he'd have to find some courage and fighting power of his own. You see, that figure ahead wasn't just another slave. The Man with the Silver Mane didn't just work with collars. It was an experiment. He didn't give it a name or a number. He called it X.

Chapter Thirty-seven

EXPERIMENT X

Experiment X was seen by some as a failure. Its hulking size made it strong. It had the weight of many, the bulk of many, and the strength of many. By some accounts—by *most* accounts—it was a monster.

But to the Man with the Silver Mane, X was no failure. X was a test. What was he trying to achieve? Oakley had scratchy memories of overheard words. He knew he was brought through the experiment chambers. He could hear the screams. No faded memory erased those.

"One body," the Magus said. "One body and many minds."

The scientists injected X with numerous substances. There was seemingly no end to the needles. Every week there was another "breakthrough," which just meant another substance, another needle. The Man with the Silver Mane claimed he was imbuing the poor soul with the souls of many other people. But not just any people. People from across the veil. People from *his* world, wherever he came from. He saw success in X's increasing size and stature. He saw the souls of many trying to burst out through its bulging muscles. All Oakley saw was the product of all those needles. There was just one soul inside, and they were killing it, day by day.

And here it was, chained, but ready to kill him today.

"Easy, now," Oakley said, as X struggled with his bonds. "Easy."

Those were words he'd say to his horses over the years. It reminded him of Old Reliable, who he'd presumed had died to the wolves. There wasn't time to ask Nox about him, and there wasn't time to hear the Coilhunter's story. Oakley had to be his own old reliable. He had to keep on trotting on.

X stared at him with frenzied eyes. Oakley wasn't quite sure if the original state of the beast was male or female. Its bulk had overcome any sense of form or figure, any indication of what it had previously been. The bulges weren't just on its body. Its face had turned into a bulbous thing with many mountains. The eyes stared out from the valleys between.

"I ain't here to hurt ya," Oakley said, holding out his hands, palms outward. He'd already placed his rifle away.

Unsurprisingly, X didn't believe him.

Nox raced through a series of doorways, taking every left he could. He passed through a room of men shovelling coal in giant, fire-licked furnaces, some with masks over their faces, some with suits covering their entire bodies, and others bare-chested, with burns and scars. They paid no heed to him, and even if they did, they were just slaves, and he was just a blur.

Yet even in the blur the Coilhunter overheard

their chatter, and gathered that the Man with the Silver Mane never went down to the furnaces. Of course, why would he? He was the master. Yet something about it stuck in Nox's mind, like the little things did during a stand-off. To him, this whole chase was the stand-off, and he was looking out for every little detail before the draw.

By now, he should've turned into the corridor leading to Porridge's ledge. But no. This fortress was built on the land, and the land was anything but cooperative. The building was as much a maze on these levels as the ones below.

Nox heard Porridge's screams. He ran to a small viewport in the wall, just barely big enough to squeeze an eyeball through. He saw the scavenger dangling. Oh, how the earth beckoned. Oh, how the ground yearned. The sky asked for nothing. All the hunger was below.

The Coilhunter tried to work out how to get to that ledge. It should've just been a few metres away, just another turn away. He scampered on, feeling for false walls, nudging against sealed hatches. A silent desperation was mounting in the back of his mind. He couldn't ask for directions. The hourglass wasn't just trickling away. It was pouring out.

Then he found it. A corridor snaked away, then led back to Porridge's ledge. He clambered through, raced to the outcrop, and pointed his arm. He had that grapnel launcher primed and ready. The ground would have to go hungry.

Then he heard the footsteps of guards behind him.

* * *

Experiment X yanked on the chains, and the walls shuddered. Oakley shook with them, though he tried to hide it. He knew to fear it instinctively, but he'd also learned to fear it from what he'd heard others say. There were reports that it had ripped scientists limb from limb, that it had popped off the heads of others like they were dolls. It might've had the souls of many, but by all accounts, there was no man or woman left in it. It was a monster. It was the Beast with No Name.

Oakley could've backed away. He could've shuffled back to the ledge and climbed back down. Part of him wanted to. Another part urged him to just race past Experiment X, to keep going, and don't look back. Fear and courage fought their war in him.

Then he heard Porridge's cries, and he knew he had to do something.

He eased up towards X, taking slow, careful steps. X watched him with those manic eyes, seizing him in their stare. Something about the look told Oakley that it could've been him. It could've been his body used. Something else told him that it still could be, that the Man with the Silver Mane would continue his experiments.

"I'm just … gonna … squeeze by," Oakley whispered.

He darted forward, summoning all his strength and speed. His heart leaped in his chest, and his head thumped to match that frantic beat.

But the Beast with No Name matched it too.

X pulled on his chains with greater force, ripping them from the walls. He swiped at Oakley, who gasped and jumped. The chain swung under his feet, but he stumbled forward and into the grasp of the monstrosity's other hand. It pushed him back and pinned him to the wall.

This is it, Oakley thought, as he wiggled and writhed. *This is what you've been searchin' for. Time to meet your maker, old boy. Time to visit the real Lostlands.*

X raised a clenched fist. Oh, the strike'd be like a meteor. It'd leave a crater in the wall and a crater in Oakley's body. Maybe it would be quick. But it wouldn't be painless.

Then X drew close, close enough that their eyes were parallel. Oakley presumed it wanted to see him truly before the kill, that it wanted to intimidate him with its horrible glare. Oakley stared back defiantly. If he was to go, he wouldn't go cowering.

Then the Beast with No Name surprised him.

It spoke.

"Help … me," it said.

Chapter Thirty-eight

FREE TO FALL

Nox shot the grapnel as he turned, gun ready in the other hand. He fired, aiming for the hip. He expected men with pistols raised. That was how it usually went in the Wild North. But no. The Man with the Silver Mane never did things the usual way. These were men in armoured suits, like something the Dew Distributors would wear, albeit with fewer sharp edges.

The bullet pinged off their armour at about the same time the grappling hook grasped the top of Porridge's collapsing ladder. Nox was pulled back a step towards the edge. Porridge still screamed.

"Well, howdy," the Coilhunter said, facing off against the guards.

"Put your weapon away," one of the guards told him. The voice was muffled just like Nox's was, but it didn't have quite so much grit.

"Which one?" Nox asked, with a glint in his eye. He slid back another centimetre.

The guards edged forward. "All of them."

They took another unified step. It was like a wall of metal, pushing Nox closer to the edge. Behind him, the grapnel pulled him too. They say most folk in the Wild North live on the edge. They weren't all daredevils and risktakers. Some were just trying to live their lives in peace, away from the war, and away from the law. But you walked a fine line in the wastes. If you were good, the bad would likely get you. And if you were bad? Well, that was where the Coilhunter came in.

Nox's eagle eyes spotted a piece of iron jutting from the ground around about where the ladder'd broken free.

"Here," Nox said, holstering his pistol. "They're all away."

He slid back again. The guards moved with him.

"The grapnel."

"It's not a weapon," Nox lied.

That helmet almost cocked. "For you, it is."

"You're right," Nox said, before wrapping the wire around the guard's neck. Then, as he felt his feet slip over the edge, pulling the guard with him, he coiled the wire around the jutting piece of iron just in time. It caught and held him there, and held the ladder from falling any further. But Porridge still dangled. It didn't matter if the Coilhunter saved the ladder. He had to save Porridge too.

The other guards raced to the edge and tried to lift up their hanging comrade. It was lucky that he wore a helmet or the wire might've sliced through his throat. But Nox wasn't here to be a hangman. There were no posters for those armoured guards, though there might've been posters for the men beneath the masks. Until he knew for certain, he couldn't kill them. Pity, that. You see, a conscience made things

… complicated.

"If you want him to live," Nox rasped, "then catch *him* over there." He nodded towards Porridge, who didn't need to be nodded to. Everyone'd spotted the multicoloured dangling man, and everyone'd heard his panicked screams echo through the chamber.

The guards pondered this for a moment, but the Coilhunter didn't have a moment to spare. He shifted the wire a little, so that it looked like it might unwind and drop the captured guard. "Hurry, now. You let that one drop, I let this one drop as well."

By rights, they should've known he wouldn't do it. He wouldn't let an innocent man fall. Not without trying to catch him. Sure, accidents happen, but everything the Coilhunter did was no accident. If there was even the hint of his hands in your death, you knew he caused it plain and simple. But those guards likely had a secret fear, likely had a secret past. The kind of past that was all too common in the Wild North. The past of a killer or a rapist. The past of a conman or a crook. Just as the Coilhunter couldn't be certain they were bad people, *they* couldn't be certain that he didn't already know they were. He wouldn't let an innocent man fall, true enough. Well, who said they were innocent?

The guards vanished back into the corridors. Maybe they were looking for help. Maybe they were looking for backup. Or maybe they'd bring both.

Nox looked at the guard flailing below him. "Let's hope you've got some friends behind those masks."

The guard said nothing. Maybe he was saving all his energy for hope.

*   *   *

Experiment X kept Oakley pinned to the wall, maybe out of instinct, maybe out of fear. After all, it was men like Oakley that'd done this to it. What, except that lost look in his eyes, would let X know that Oakley was any different?

"What can I do?" Oakley asked.

"Free ... me."

"How?"

X shook its head, then punched the wall beside Oakley. The drifter hoped to God it was intentional, because he didn't like the idea that the creature missed.

"I tried," X said, pointing to a variety of scars on its body. One of them was a complete laceration around its throat. It was clear by those scars, but also by that desperate, defeated look in its eyes, that it had tried many times to kill itself.

"What happened?" Oakley asked.

"He ... keeps ... bringin' ... me back." Its voice was low and laboured, its breathing heavy and difficult. Its body didn't just bulge outwards. It bulged inwards as well, right into its own organs. Those experiments were slowly killing it, and yet the Man with the Silver Mane just wouldn't let it die.

"How?" Oakley wondered. He'd heard a lot of tales about the afterlife on his travels, and some folk believed you had a chance of coming back. He'd explored the teachings of so many sects and tribes, he wasn't sure what to believe. All he knew for sure was that Experiment X was in a kind of pain he had never experienced himself. They say it can always get better.

Well, it could always get worse.

"I … don't know."

Oakley shook his head and mused. If the Man with the Silver Mane was a Magus, then it was possible he had some control of unseen forces. That was just a rumour though. If anything, the supposed Magi seemed like everybody else. They had a mystique about them, sure. They gained a reputation with their consecration of amulets for the Order. Some of them, like Doctor Mudro, did a little bit of stage magic on the side. But otherwise they were just flesh and blood. The Regime had made an example of enough of them to prove that.

"So … much … pain," X said.

Oakley could see it clearly. Even now, those muscles didn't just bulge, but seemed to pulse and bubble, as if there was something horrible beneath the skin. At times the flesh went so red Oakley thought there might be lava underneath. What was certain was that with so much pain and pressure, X was a volcano waiting to explode.

The Coilhunter dangled, the guard dangled, and Porridge dangled. Some folk said that's all you did in the Wild North. You clung on helplessly to the fraying thread of life. And boy did they cling.

Nox wasn't sure what the guards'd do. Maybe they hadn't gone for help, like he hoped, and were just leaving them all to hang, like flies caught in the web. Or maybe they were an efficient kind and would let gravity do all the work. Maybe the guard below Nox had no friends at all.

Then the Coilhunter heard a commotion below,

and he saw many people assembling something at the corners of the chamber. It seemed like maybe it was a net of sorts. Except Nox couldn't see a net. Maybe they were just there to watch them fall.

Agonising minutes passed, and you could sure as hell bet they felt like hours. It's strange what goes through folks' heads at times like that. More often than not, it's bad things. See, it wasn't enough to fall and die. Your mind had to play it out before it happened. In that way, your mind became an accomplice of your fate.

But even in the Wild North, miracles happen. Sometimes folk do good. Sometimes, just sometimes, you don't fall.

The people below finished their placement, hammered some buttons, pulled some levers, and then a force field formed between their erected barrier. That was something to see, if you could see it, as it was only in the periodic glimmer that you could, but it was no help lying on the ground. It was lucky, then, that there were pneumatic pistons in the pieces the guards had placed. They slowly pushed the force field higher, until it was just about within reach of all those dangling feet. It was good timing, because that was when Porridge's grasp faltered. It was a short drop, but that didn't stop the scavenger from shrieking.

"Oh! I'm done for!" He rolled about on the force field as if he was still in mid fall. It took a while for him to fully fathom that he'd already landed, and that he'd landed sooner than he expected. The force field shimmered as he moved.

With Porridge safe, Nox was able to let himself and the guard down—but he kept *his* guard up. He let the grapnel hook back into place, then waited with Porridge as the pneumatic pistons lowered the energy platform.

"How is it you keep fallin'?" Nox asked.

"How is it you keep catching me?" Porridge replied with a smile.

"Well, this time, I didn't."

"In a roundabout way, you did, dearie. Oh! It's not like *they* would catch a little old dandy like me of their own accord." He cast a dirty look at the guard Nox freed. That man kept himself as far away from them as he could.

"You never know," Nox said. "For all that standin' out you do, you sure have a way of fittin' in."

"Maybe it's the collar," Porridge suggested. "Though I do wonder how we'll fit in now."

They reached ground level, where they were greeted by several dozen armed guards. Those guards wore collars too. It seemed that the Man with the Silver Mane didn't have many people on his side that weren't slaves. No wonder he wanted to leave.

"Hands in the air," a female guard, wearing similar armour to the others, said. They only knew she was female because she had her helmet under her arm. Her black hair was cut tight, but she had a soft face to parry her hard eyes.

Porridge flung his arms up like he was praising God. Nox raised his slowly, perhaps because he didn't feel like praising. A lot slower than the guard wanted if that glare was anything to go by. When the

Coilhunter did things slow, you watched every aching moment of it, because normally he did things so fast you didn't catch it 'til he caught you. So you watched the slow motion, because it was like seeing how the magic tricks were done. Yeah, Nox could be his own kind of magician.

"What shall we call you this time?" the woman asked. "Hookdangler? Wirewalker?"

Nox shrugged his shoulders, and he made a show of it too. "How's about you call me the Man Who Killed the Man with the Silver Mane."

"How droll. Shall we carve it on your grave?"

Nox smirked. "So long as you carve it on his first."

"Don't worry," she said, and she smiled back. "That'll be a long day off. We're gonna make you two work 'til you drop. You're part of the machine now. His Eminence will be glad to have a few more cogs."

The guards crowded in now. Nox could've tried to fight them, but there were a few too many, and the Coilhunter was saving his mojo for the Magus upstairs. Nox'd have to wait for a more opportune moment. Besides, if they were to be cogs, then they'd be the cogs that jammed the machine.

Chapter Thirty-nine

EXPERIMENT NOX

The female guard, whom Nox overheard was called Yilda, led them through many corridors and up many stairs, with a long trail of guards behind them. Nox spotted periodic opportunities to escape or attack, but so long as Yilda was leading them upwards—to where he could feel that mounting presence—he decided he'd hold off for now. You see, the best gunslingers waited for the perfect moment. They didn't draw too early or too late. Death wasn't the only perfectionist.

And that perfect moment arrived now.

The Coilhunter heard the buzz of electricity ahead and to the left. It was another generator. By anyone's guess, that fortress must've had dozens of them. And who knew what the Man with the Silver Mane was doing with harnessed lightning at the peak.

Nox flicked a butterfly capsule from his belt, which rolled ahead of Yilda. It was empty, one of the ones that needed a refill, but it caused a panic all the same. Simultaneously, he hit a switch on the steel-plated guitar on his back, which unleashed a thick smog into the corridor. They say in situations like that, all hell breaks loose—but if you're already in

Hell, well, then where does it break loose from?

With all the commotion, Nox slipped into the generator room and sealed the door. Sure, he could've tried to pull Porridge in, but that scavenger'd have to be a pawn in the game for now. So long as they had one of them, they thought they had both. And that'd be true if they had the Coilhunter. Right now, they had nothing.

"Beat the door down!" Yilda yelled.

And they tried.

They hammered their fists against it. They bashed their boots against it. They slammed their shoulders against it. The beat increased, from a pitter-patter percussion to a rumbling, roaring, rolling barrage.

And still the door held.

They should've known it would hold, because they'd made it. They made it to last. They made it to survive the Coilhunter. It was the common, cruel irony of the Wild North that what you made would unmake you.

"He better not destroy that generator," Yilda warned Porridge, "or we'll be forced to destroy you."

She said it loud enough for all to hear—for the Coilhunter to hear. That told him well enough that it was an idle threat. The thing is, when left alone for long enough, such threats have a way of becoming not so idle.

"Oh! Don't panic me, sweetie! Oh, I'm seeing stars! Oh!"

Porridge promptly fainted on the spot, though he made sure to hobble over to some guards so that he could conveniently slump into their arms, and thereby rend them armless in a battle. It was one hell of a defence mechanism, and the fact that he'd survived the Wild North to date showed just how well it worked. They say you should feign death. Well, fainting worked too.

"Bring in the Lightning Ram," Yilda ordered.

It took them a while, but when they brought it, Porridge couldn't help but pry one eye open just a little. The battering ram was about the size of a man, rectangular in shape, with a large copper prong down the centre, and a capstone of silver formed into the shape of a ram's head. It even had little lightning bolts for ears. Yeah, who said you couldn't break down doors with style? Porridge might've even applauded them, if he weren't too busy applauding his own performance.

"Knock it down," Yilda said.

They struck the door with the ram, and it didn't just shake—it crackled. Each strike released a blast of electricity, which expanded outwards across the entire door. Just like everything in the Man with the Silver Mane's arsenal, he had to augment it with lightning.

So, working frantically inside the room to the beats and the booms, so did Nox.

With a few more heaves, the door finally blasted open. The smoke and dust hung in the air for a moment, and everyone outside held their breaths. There was a lot of nervous fidgeting with weapons, a lot of sharp and swift glances at shadows, a lot of racing minds playing out every grim scenario.

Well, none of them played out this.

When Nox appeared in the haze, there was something different about him. He had a new arsenal of his own. He still had his grapnels, but he'd augmented them with power rods, so that he could electrify the wire at the flick of a switch. He now wore a pair of arm-length rubber gloves he'd taken from the generator room's supply, which helped protect him from any inadvertent shock of his own.

He fired the right grapnel, and the guards thought he'd missed, and unwisely tugged on the wire. When he gave them a jolt, and they fell to the ground, sizzling, a new kind of panic swept through the others like a current.

"He's charged his grapnels!" one of the guards shouted.

But that wasn't all he'd done.

He marched out into the corridor, casting metal orbs across the floor in either direction. They exploded, releasing a new kind of shrapnel the guards'd never seen before. They were a kind of electrified throwing star, which shocked their target on impact. They each had little power rods of their own. Nox'd wrapped them in metal sheeting and bashed them into the shape of a five-pointed star, the signature emblem of a sheriff.

He didn't have time to paint on the five colours he'd assigned to the various groups he deemed as threats: red for the tribesfolk, blue for the bikers, green for the criminals, yellow for the Clockwork Commune, and black for the so-called demons of the Regime. At first there were no colours. Then the colours meant something else. For a while, it was just four points, before Nox recognised that it was only a matter of time before the Regime moved in on the Wild North. They'd earned their colour. Black would oppose them. He wondered when he'd have to make it six.

Some guards fought, but most of them just scattered, and they left behind the ram. It was one thing to fight the Coilhunter, but to fight an augmented Coilhunter was something else. It was like facing the Man with a Thousand Names and the Man with the Silver Mane all at once.

Guards toppled like dominoes. Nox was able to take them out in twos and threes, then half a dozen at a time. And it was the way he wanted to do it. He got to save his bullets for those who deserved it. For now, all he had to do was send these guards off to a shock-filled sleep. He marched through the corridors, firing grapnels and releasing them, and rolling more star-filled orbs into the fleeing crowd. He followed them into a large room, where he swung a cast grapnel hook around like a lasso, then a flail. He took them down by the dozen then, until all he faced was Yilda herself.

If Yilda'd had a pistol, she would've unloaded it now until she clicked empty. But you see, before now there was no need for pistols. The slaves came willingly, and the guards kept everyone alive as part of the machine. Everyone feared the Man with the Silver Mane. Everyone but Nox.

Yilda stumbled over the bodies of her guards as she stepped backwards.

"You'll pay a heavy price!" she shouted. "You'll—"

But Nox cast a grapnel her way, and gave her a jolt that silenced her.

"You've got it wrong, girl," Nox rasped. "Folk pay me."

With the echoes of the screams and zaps now faded, Porridge pushed a few bodies off him and dusted himself off. He skipped after the Coilhunter, hopping between the snoozing guards.

"Phew!" Porridge cried. "We're safe. Oh!"

Nox instinctively grumbled. If there was anything he'd learned in the Wild North, it was that there was no such thing as safe. The land wouldn't let you. The sun wouldn't let you. The animals and people wouldn't let you. Even in the grave you weren't safe. No wonder the Man with the Silver Mane wanted to escape.

Then, just on cue, they heard a clatter of iron chains. Large metal doors screeched open. Behind them came a kind of flood. Not of water, that ever-so-rare and ever-so-costly liquid. No, this was a flood of flesh. This was a crowding, crushing cluster of slaves. They all wore collars. Some of them wore chains. All of them had a look of grim determination to stop the Coilhunter.

Chapter Forty

FLOOD

A flood wasn't something you saw in the Wild North. The rivers ran dry. The parched earth cracked. The rain came seldom, and more often than not came at the behest of certain tribes—or so they said. The Dew Distributors'd staked claims to every patch of water they could find, and if you found a patch yourself, well, they'd claim you.

So, when the Coilhunter thought of those slaves as pouring in like a flood, it was an image that carried a lot of weight. It was the image of three hundred slaves let loose from the dam of their prison doors. It was the image of a madman's hold on the minds of many, used like a weapon against the minds of the few.

"Out of the frying pan," Porridge said, "and into the—"

"Not fire," Nox said. No. This was water. He remembered the feeling at the campfire, when the fire drowned out the presence of the Man with the Silver Mane. That Magus chose electricity for his weapon, and, sure enough, that was its own kind of fire— the so-called "astral fire" of the tribes. But it wasn't the same. Real fire had a different burn. Nox, of all people, knew that well.

But if this was to be a flood, then there was one thing the Coilhunter knew well about water. You kept it far away from electricity.

Nox hammered the buttons that electrified his grapnels. Both of them sizzled and sparked. He held out his arms and circled on the spot, making sure each and every one of those slaves knew what he had. They *feared* that all-too-familiar shock. Nox knew that too. But if both their master and their enemy wielded it, what would they do?

"Back off," Nox growled.

The slaves considered this. In the eyes of some, who had spent far longer in the grasp of the Man with the Silver Mane, they looked at the Coilhunter now as a new kind of master. After all, he had mastered that chaotic energy. That must've made him special. In the eyes of most, though, was the reflection of the eyes of their true master. They saw nothing but the object of their orders.

They stepped in a little. Nox saw it as the waters rising.

"Oh! What are we to do, cabbage?" Porridge whimpered. "We'll never fight them all!"

Nox knew that well. For every slave he could count, there were a dozen more huddled behind. Even with his gadgets, he couldn't take them all down. Pretty soon they were all going to drown.

Then they heard a roar from the rafters, and all eyes turned to see the colossal form of Experiment X on one of the iron platforms there. No, not just Experiment X. Oakley too.

They got 'im was Nox's first thought, until he saw Oakley cling onto X's back as it climbed down to join them. That wasn't just a monster. That wasn't just a slave.

It was backup.

"Nice of you to finally join us," Nox said.

"I was a little … caught up," Oakley replied.

They tried not to stare at X, but that beast must've been used to stares. That was just another emotional pain to add to the physical torment. But you see, Oakley was different. Oakley did what no one else'd do. He gave that beast a chance.

"This one wants to be free," Oakley said.

"That's good," Nox said, "but those ones don't."

It seemed Oakley hadn't quite taken in just how many slaves had leaked into the room, because he did a double-take when he saw them. The flood had virtually surrounded them.

"Well, drifter," Oakley said. "There's worse ways to die."

Porridge mouthed the word *die* and almost keeled over.

Nox turned on the spot, taking in as much of his surroundings as possible. "We ain't dyin' yet."

The first wave of slaves was close enough to almost crash upon their shore. Fists formed. Fingers hovered over weapons. Eyes settled like arrows on their prey. This would be a battle of slave against slave. All of them ran a nervous finger inside their collars.

But, like many battles, you could count on things not going the way you expected. You could count on outside influences. You could count on late arrivals.

They heard a bang from the giant door across the way. All eyes turned. The pre-battle eye-squinting and finger-fidgeting froze for a moment. Everyone waited to see who it was knocking loudly on the door. No, it couldn't be Experiment X. That beast was inside. Whatever this was, it wasn't a slave.

Then the door burst open, and they saw a horse rearing. The sunlight gleamed off its iron legs. The sunlight also revealed the horse's companions: a clockwork construct and a toy duck.

Chapter Forty-one

BACKUP

When Duck waddled into the room, the Coilhunter knew one thing for certain. Things were going to get bright.

"Here," Nox said, hurriedly pulling out some spare goggles. "You'll need these."

"I've got my own, thank you, peach." Porridge unearthed goggles with a bright floral pattern. They didn't go with anything else he was wearing, but when nothing matches, everything matches.

Oakley took a pair from Nox and put them on. "Never did like goggles," he grumbled as he fought with the strap. "Sometimes you get stuck in your ways."

Nox twisted a dial on the side of his own goggles, which put a black shutter down behind the glass. "Yeah," he said. "And sometimes you adapt."

It was then that Duck halted, glanced around the room, and gave that familiar, ominous little "Quack."

Everything went a brilliant, burning white for those who weren't wearing blackout goggles. The boom was like thunder. People fell or fled, thinking a bomb'd just gone off. It had, but this one wasn't packed with shrapnel. It was packed with light.

"Now," Nox said. "This is where the fun begins."

The slaves might've been blinded, but with the eyes of the Man with the Silver Mane behind them, they could still kind of see. They charged in, swinging chains and brandishing daggers and cleavers. Nox fired his electrified grappling hooks and spun them wildly. Almost simultaneously, he cast capsules and orbs this way and that, releasing butterflies on one side and electrified sheriff stars on the other. Folk fell by the dozen, you could bet the animals they were dreaming of weren't sheep.

Old Reliable charged in, running down slaves in his path. He reared and kicked and bucked, tossing people in all directions. More than anything, he looked for Oakley in the battle and cleared a path to him. He nudged his master gently, let him climb on board, and then returned to the fight.

Duck'd done his part, and it'd be a while before he'd recharge his weapon. But that didn't stop him chasing a few slaves here and there. It must've been quite a sight to see, if it wasn't for the chaos of it all.

Bitnickle was an adventurer, but not much of a fighter. What she did do, though, was provide a distraction. She played clips of audio from various radio stations across Altadas, mostly from the Regime and the gang lords of the Wild North.

"Stop what you're doing," her radio crackled. And some of the slaves stopped, because it was the voice of the Iron Emperor, whose hypnotic brogue was even more powerful than that of the Man with the Silver Mane. While the slaves were dazed, Duck waddled between them, carrying a wire in his mouth. When the slaves came out of their stupor, they tripped and tumbled on the spot. Well, when you brought toys to the battle, you could expect them to play games.

Porridge was forced to fight hand-to-hand with the slaves, and boy did he fight. He wrestled and tossed them to the ground, or he was tossed to the ground himself. All to a flurry of creative insults— but not a "plum" or "peach" in sight. At times, the Coilhunter rolled through, taking down a fighter here and there. At other times, Experiment X thundered through, taking down a dozen fighters.

By the end of it, most of the slaves lay prone, while a handful of others retreated back to their cells. It wasn't fear that made them retreat. The Man with the Silver Mane did it. He didn't need them anymore. He'd delayed the Coilhunter long enough.

"I think that should do it," Oakley said, nodding to all the writhing, groaning bodies.

"No," Nox said, letting the grapnels lock back into place. He looked at the stairway leading up to the higher levels. "There's still one more man to beat."

Chapter Forty-two

THE MAN WITH
THE SILVER MANE

Porridge stayed with Old Reliable, Duck, and Bitnickle, keeping guard, while the others followed the many, winding steps up to the High Chambers, where the presence of the Man with the Silver Mane was palpable. The door was open. This time.

They entered, but they kept a safe distance. They got just close enough to see their captor's face, to see those shimmering eyes. They tried not to stare, but they couldn't help it. After all, they were still slaves. Behind the Magus was a large oval, mechanical frame, held up by ropes, held to the ground by more ropes, and fed with wires that connected to the many generators of the fortress. Further behind, there was the periodic blast of lightning off an energy collector. God only knew how that was caused, or maybe God was causing it himself.

Strangest of all, which was saying something, the Man with the Silver Mane wore a slave collar too. That unsettled the Coilhunter more than anything, because it made him wonder if this face on the poster of his mind was really the man in charge. Well, some said God was the man in charge. If he was in charge of this, then Nox'd have to gun him down too.

"Nathaniel Osley Xander," the Man with the Silver Mane crooned. "Good old Nox. Or is it Coilhunter? I never could keep up with all your names."

"And what's yours, Magus?"

"It's of no importance here, though I hear you call me the Man with the Silver Mane. Where's the poster for me, Coilhunter? Ah, I see. You've chiselled it on your brain."

"Well, if I have to hand in my brain to cash you in," Nox said, "then gimme somethin' to scoop it out."

"How crude, Coilhunter. I see you're more brawn than brains. There are better, more cultured ways to achieve our ends. Of course, the Wild North is not the place for them, now, is it? Why, Altadas as a whole is so devoid of culture. You can save those caches in the sea and sky, but at the end of the day you're all just animals."

"So, what, you give us dog collars?"

The Magus scoffed. "You have no idea, do you? Ah, so focused on these wars of yours. If you paid heed to the other worlds out there, you might see there are *other* ways. But I will educate you yet. I will feed your brain like a pig. I'll fatten it up so we can harness more from it."

"You're makin' me hungry," Nox said.

"Oh, back to basics with you, I see. I should've known when I let you return."

"*Let* me? I didn't see many open doors."

"We closed them so *you* would open them."

"Why not just let me in then? Why make me

fight?"

"Isn't it obvious? It's the fight that does it, Nox. It's the emotion of it all. It's fuel. It's energy. Those collars aren't to make you slaves. No. They're harnesses, to harness that raw passion inside of you. The electricity is just one source of power. To open this portal, I needed every source I could find. Did you not realise that humans are the most potent source of all?"

"And here I was thinking they were just people," Nox said.

"For a toymaker, you have so little imagination."

"Is that so, huh? Well, I can imagine you dead."

"And that's all it'll be, Coilhunter. A figment of your imagination."

"It ends here. This prison of yours. This fantasy."

"It's not a fantasy," the Man with the Silver Mane said. "I'll make a believer out of you yet."

The Magus shocked him. Nox grunted and fell to one knee.

"Each time you fear, each time you anger, each time you hurt, you generate more of that power."

Nox gritted his teeth behind his mask. He tried not to show his fear, or his anger, or his pain. He tried to bury it all deep down inside him, where he buried his love for his family, where the Man with the Silver Mane would never find it.

But he found it.

"So much buried emotion," the Magus said. "You've stored it all in you like a battery. There's so much power there, if we can just release it."

"Let him go," Oakley said, stepping forward.

The Magus shocked him too, and he fell.

Experiment X backed off.

"And you," the Magus said, turning his gaze on Oakley. "Not quite so deep, but still buried. Men's emotions are like dynamite, all wrapped up in neat little cylinders, just waiting for someone to light the fuse."

"So, what are we, batteries or explosives?" Nox asked.

"Both. In the grand scheme of things, they all generate the necessary power. Even now you are generating it." There was a manic glee in his eyes. "I shall harness it. I shall harness you all!"

"Even with a bullet in your head?"

Nox fired, but the bullet pinged off an energy shield around the Magus.

"Go on," the Man with the Silver Mane said. "Power me further."

But the Coilhunter refrained. There was no point wasting bullets. That Magus might've lost his magic when he came to Altadas, but he hadn't lost his mind. He'd created new things that mimicked the magic of old. He wielded science like a wand.

For Nox and his companions, this was a moment of quandary. Here they were, at the pinnacle of the world, at the doorstep of defeating their captor. But the question was: if fighting him only made him stronger, then how would they defeat him?

Chapter Fourty-three

PROMISED PORTALS

Well, the Coilhunter had a hunch.

Nox took a box of matches from his belt and rolled it between his fingers. Instantly he could see the Man with the Silver Mane's eyes light up. Nox struck a match.

"What?" the Magus asked. "You want to light the fuse yourself?"

Nox smiled. "You'd light it with electricity. But I've got a different spark here, and I know you fear it."

The Magus guffawed loudly. "I do not fear a flame."

"What about a fire?"

The Magus said nothing.

Nox took a step forward with that burning match. The Magus took a step back.

"Tell me you're not afraid," Nox said.

The Magus zapped him. "I'm not afraid," he growled.

Nox struggled back up and took another step forward, lighting another match. The Magus shrank back again and jolted him.

"I'm not afraid."

And again Nox fought forward, fighting through

the pain. If the Magus truly knew him, he should've known that he would fight through anything. He'd already fought through the fire before. Now it was time to bring back the flame.

"You're only feeding me," the Magus warned. "The portal will be ready soon."

And that might've been true, but the Coilhunter wanted to feed him something a little hot. He wasn't sure what it was about the fire that overcame him. That was an energy source too, but he didn't use it. He feared it.

And Nox kept pushing forward.

So, the Man with the Silver Mane set his eyes upon Experiment X, who baulked in his presence. X might've had its own anger burning deep inside it, but it also had fear. More than anything or anyone, it knew what the Magus could do, what it *had* done. It knew it could not resist him. It knew it had to fight too.

Experiment X bounded up after the Coilhunter and pinned him to the ground.

"No!" Oakley shouted, but the Magus zapped him too. "Fight it! Fight *him*!"

"Enough of your games, Coilhunter," the Magus said. "Let me show you what I can do."

He showed him an image in his mind of another portal. Nox gazed through it, and there, on the other side—just an arm stretch away—was his family. There she was, beloved Emma. There she was, little gentle Ambrose. And there he was, little wild Aaron. Not tombstones. Not cracked earth. There they were in the flesh.

For a moment, for a lifetime, Nox held his breath. It was their lifetimes, so he didn't hold it for long. The gunslinger in him faded, and he found the husband, found the father. He wanted to run to them, wanted to pick them up, wanted to hold them in his arms. For so many nights, all he held were his guns. No matter how tightly he gripped them, it didn't help him let go of the pain.

"It's … not real," he said.

"It's as real as you want it to be."

"Is that all your portal is, then? A lie?"

"No," the Man with the Silver Mane said. "It's very much the truth."

"But this," Nox said, "this image you show me. It's just a mirage."

"And will you not quench your thirst in this oasis?"

"But it's a lie."

"Everything is a lie, if you look at it a certain way. And everything's the truth, if you look at it from another. That's what the Magi learn, that all is a paradox, that everything is and isn't. Won't you look at your family and see them alive? If they walk this earth again with you, what would you do?"

Nox was caught up in the thought of it. He imagined holding their hands, kissing their cheeks, and hugging them tight. He imagined telling them he loved them, that they meant more to him than anything in this world or any other. He imagined showing them his love, spending every waking moment with them, and dreaming of them in his sleep.

He imagined.

"It's not real," he repeated. He'd honed his mind for this, even though he didn't want to accept it. He trained with the mirages of the desert. Early on, he'd thought he'd seen his family in the distance, but the closer he got, the farther away they seemed. He was chasing phantoms, like he was once chasing ghosts with Taberah Cotten of the Resistance. He had to let them go.

"Give in to it," the Magus said. "For once, just stop fighting and give in to your ideal version of the truth. You will find peace."

But Nox was more lucid now. The anger rooted him back in the moment.

"And what about this world?" he asked. "What about peace here?"

The Magus scoffed. "There will never be peace."

"Well, you're right there," Nox said. "Not with people like you."

"I'm not the one fighting, Coilhunter. You are. And what a pretty war you've raged. Do you think you will ever *allow* peace to happen? The hunt, the kill, the battle—it's everything you live for. It's the *only* thing you live for. You don't even live for them anymore."

That was enough to cause the dynamite to explode. Nox roared and fought with Experiment X. They struggled and they screamed. The room buzzed with the subtle energy of the fight.

"Yes," the Magus said. "It's happening."

Inside the oval frame, the portal opened. It was a swirling blueish-white energy, like a different kind of electricity, like perhaps the kind that crackled across the skies of the Magus' homeworld. Through that strange looking-glass, all eyes could see a different place, a place of green fields, a place of rivers and rain.

So different to Altadas. So different to the Wild North.

No wonder he wanted to go back there.

Chapter Forty-four

GOING HOME

"I'm going home," the Man with the Silver Mane said softly. Soft enough that maybe he didn't quite believe it.

He took an unsteady step forward, like a child learning to walk—like a child preparing to run to his mother's arms. There was an unlocked innocence in him now, devoid of all his adult machinations, devoid of all his scheming, all his manipulation and torture. In the moment of it all, he was made anew.

"Home," he repeated, even softer. All the power and menace of his voice was gone. All the grit dissolved into a calm and tender resonance. In the word he spoke, and the way he said it, was the memory of his mother, the warmth of the hearth, and the feeling of having a place in the world. Who wouldn't want that? Who wouldn't yearn for that? Who wouldn't find any way possible to make it true?

"I see it," he whispered. Tears flooded his face, a mirror of the rivers in the world he saw, where there were green pastures, and green forests—where there was magic. But then maybe life was magic. There was so much life there.

He stepped closer to the portal, so close to home

now. There was something kind of beautiful about it, about someone so long stranded finally getting to see their home again, finally getting to return to what they must've thought was unreturnable. He was the real Lostlander, and now he'd been found. Now he was going home.

Except the Coilhunter was there.

Nox dragged himself onwards, finger by finger, inch by inch, until he could reach out towards the nearest rope. He struck a match and let it burn. The fire snaked its way up towards the portal, where something sparked, and the entire frame went ablaze. The flames licked the swirling mass, so that to pass through one would mean passing through the other.

"No!" the Magus screamed. He tried to move towards the portal, but backed away instead. Inside him was the battle between hope and fear, that same battle that so many faced, played out so forcefully now.

The flames engulfed the portal, and the shimmering doorway flickered. It wasn't clear which would fade first, the fire or the portal.

Nox couldn't afford to wait.

He took a capsule from his belt and slammed it against Experiment X's ear. It was a sound charge, which sent an ear-rending boom into the creature's brain. It stumbled off him, giving him just enough time to hit the smoke button on his guitar. He vanished into the haze, which was common for the Coilhunter, but this time he tried something new. He took the guitar off and swung it to the side, snapping a lever behind the neck. When the guitar skidded to a halt, the body swung open and up popped a scarecrow in the image of the Coilhunter. It didn't quite do him justice, but in the smog it looked like him just fine.

As X bounded after the fake Coilhunter, the real Nox charged towards the Man with the Silver Mane, casting smoke canisters in all directions. He knew he couldn't penetrate the energy shield around the Magus, couldn't shoot or punch him, couldn't even move him. But he could goad him with fire.

Mid-run, Nox swept his coat off and set it ablaze. He swung it by the Magus, who backed away in terror. He should've known he was safe inside his shield, that the flames couldn't hurt him, but fear is a terrible thing. Fear consumes and crumbles. Fear is the magician that makes a million horrible mirages. Fear is what destroys lives, what kills futures, what makes strong folk weak. And Fear was another name they gave the Coilhunter.

The Man with the Silver Mane backed away, hands held out, warding off that frightening fire. He was a broken man, whose silver hair now faded to grey, whose gemstone eyes now turned to the glistening eyes of the lost and the hopeless.

Again the Coilhunter flashed the flames at him, even as it consumed his coat and threatened to consume him too. He ushered the Magus away, back, another step, another yard, another footfall, even as the lightning flashed behind him.

Then Experiment X came back into the fight, holding the severed scarecrow head. He ran for the Coilhunter, but Oakley charged into his path, blocking the way.

"No!" Oakley shouted. "I gave you a chance!"

"Move!" X roared. "Or I move you!"

"You wanted to be free! This is how! Give *this* a chance."

X struggled with its thoughts, and then struggled with the electrical lash of the Man with the Silver Mane. It had endured so much. Could it not endure just a little longer?

And then, with one final sweep of the burning rag, the Coilhunter pushed that opposing king into place. It wasn't just checkmate. This was where the crown tumbled by its own hand. The lightning struck again, and this time it struck the shield around the Magus. The blast was like a bomb, and it would've killed him were it not for that shield. It didn't kill him, but it broke the shell around him.

With his defences gone, and with the fire in Nox's hand now charred to embers, the Man with the Silver Mane made one last-ditch effort to run towards the portal. The flames there were fading too, and though the portal itself flickered, the doorway still held for now.

But just as the Magus placed his hand through the shimmering portal, just as he was about to be free of this world of exile, there was a sound like bouncing springs. He looked down, and he saw the Coilhunter's grapnel around his left ankle.

"No," he said, shaking his head slowly. He tried desperately now to push onwards through the portal, but the wire went taut. On the other end across the room, the Coilhunter started to reel him in.

"Finally you say somethin' right," he croaked.

"*No.* No, you ain't goin'. No, you ain't leavin'. No, you ain't gettin' away with this."

"Please!" the Magus begged. "Please just let me go!"

"But you said it," the Coilhunter replied. "Your magic word: *No.*"

"All I wanted was to go back!"

"And you know what? I might've helped you, if you'd have gone about it another way. But you committed great crimes here. You committed atrocities. I can't let you go away unpunished. I can't *inflict* you on some other world, even if it is your own. Maybe they sent you here wrongly, or maybe they sent you here as a punishment. Sent you to Hell. Well, you can climb and crawl, but you ain't gettin' outta here. You ain't goin' to Heaven."

Nox unloaded every bullet he had left in his guns, until the Man with the Silver Mane coughed up blood. It didn't matter what he did now. It didn't matter if he got home. With those wounds, he'd quickly find another place to be.

"Why fire?" Nox asked him, aware that he might not learn the answer. It was a question he sometimes asked himself. *Why did they have to die to fire?* He hated the flames, like he hated the criminals of the Wild North. But that didn't mean he wouldn't use them.

"That's … how … they killed me," the Magus said. "Burned … at the stake. Arlin had no … place for magic. We were … sent oversea … or burned."

"But you're alive," Nox said, aware that it was only for so long.

The Magus tapped the amulet around his neck, the so-called Beldarian the Magi used in their homeworld. "My soul … in here. My companion … he brought it here … when he was exiled. He does not … fear the fire."

"Your companion," Nox said. "Who is he?"

"Break it," the Magus said, tapping the amulet again. "Don't let him … bring me back again. Not here. Not …"

His words trailed out, and his breath went with them. His eyes stared, unblinking, and they looked a little bit more crystalline than before. His skin too was different, harsher, with a darker hue, like he was carved out of rock. For the first time, it seemed like he was not a man at all. But mirages showed you a lot of things.

Nox smashed the *beldar* jewel in the Magus' amulet, and a purple dust sprayed into the air. When it faded, the presence of the Magus was finally and completely gone.

With the Man with the Silver Mane now dead, the slave collars clicked open, including his own. It wasn't clear what powered them. It wasn't clear what bound them together. All that was clear was that the Magus' grasp was over, that they were free.

"This ends here," Nox said. "This technology too." He pulled the power units from his grapnel launchers and stomped on them. "Let it die with him."

After they departed and were long out of view, a figure emerged from the shadows. It was the Gravedigger. He slumped over the ruined form of the Man with the Silver Mane.

"So much wasted energy," he said. "What to do with it?" He smiled. "Don't you know, Coilhunter, that nothing ever truly dies?"

Chapter Forty-five

THE LONG ROAD SOUTH

With the slaves free, they made a bonfire of collars in the largest chamber. They burned, and the fact that it was fire was more fitting than they realised. All they knew was that the Man with the Silver Mane had perished, and that the Coilhunter was the man who'd killed him. They left the details to Death, who guarded them jealously.

There was one collar that was larger than the rest. Oakley placed it on the pyre. Experiment X had fought on both sides of the battle, and so, in many ways, had they all. When the portal finally faded, that beast faded with it. It wasn't clear if those many souls inside it went back to their homeworld, or if that one soul'd just hung on long enough to see its master toppled.

They scoured the fortress, all levels of it, to make sure there weren't any more trapped slaves. When they found the room with the hamster wheel, they didn't find the wolves. What's more, no one'd even heard of them. Were it not for the wounds inflicted on Old Reliable, Nox might've thought them an illusion. Unsurprisingly, the Back Door Guard were also gone, though the Coilhunter had no doubts about them.

There were some who talked about the potential of the Magus' technology, but Nox'd have none of it. He'd already seen how dangerous it was. He could see more danger in the greedy eyes of others. He destabilised the power generators and destroyed what he could. He knew, in time, the whole castle would come tumbling down. That's why you didn't make a castle of sand.

He met Rassa again, who didn't fight him now, which was good, because then the Coilhunter didn't have to fight back. Rassa returned the monowheel, which was in mostly good condition, though Nox knew he'd have to remove those glass windows on the sides.

"You're free now," Nox said.

"We were always free," Rassa said. "Freer than you. That's what it means to be lost. Let no worries find you."

The repairs to the Dandyman took some time, but many of the slaves—including those who'd worked as scientists and engineers for the Man with the Silver Mane—lent their aid where they could. Throughout the repairs, Porridge was seen in five different outfits, though no one had ever seen him change.

"Well, plum," the scavenger said to Nox as they toiled together. Duck watched the repairs blankly. "That was quite a journey. Oh! Remind me never to play with magicians. Oh, my spinning cogs!"

"We did it," Nox said, "but we've still got some journeying left to do."

They voyaged south, out of the crumbling shadow

of the castle of sand. There was one final strike of lightning, which this time almost seemed to travel up instead of down. Then the fortress faded into the sandy haze, and all folk, lost and found, went their separate ways.

It took several days to pass the unmarked barrier between the Lostlands and the other, vast stretches of the Wild North. They could feel the passage with the signposts of their hearts. The air grew crisper. The sand seemed to soften. Of course, it wouldn't be long before they'd adjust and grow tired of that as well. The sand is always softer on the other side.

"Well," Nox said, riding in his monowheel beside Oakley. "Did you find what you were lookin' for?"

"Not quite," the drifter said, and he patted Old Reliable's mane. "But I found somethin' alright. I found folk who had it far worse than me. Doesn't entirely absolve my troubles, mind, but I guess I found some appreciation for the things I've got. Sometimes we focus so much on what we've lost, we forget what we have. Well, shucks, I've got my freedom, and that's a hell of a lot more than some."

"Thank the heavens we were able to free the others!" Porridge shouted down from the Dandyman, which hovered close to the sand. "Oh! And thank us, peaches! Thank us!"

"What gets me," Oakley said, "is that I think this is just a grain of sand in a bigger desert. These aren't the only slaves out there. There are so many gangs and groups stealin' the liberty of good folk."

"We'll get to them," Nox promised.

"Perhaps, Nathaniel, but it seems like we're just a

grain of sand too."

Nox's eyes lit up. "Well, look what a grain did."

Chapter Forty-six

FAMILIAR SANDS

Porridge parted away with the others, telling them he needed a long holiday and a long, hot soak in a bath. They said their goodbyes, but they didn't make much of them, because they had that gunslinger gut feeling that they'd see each other again pretty soon.

Oakley joined the Coilhunter for a time, telling him he was happy for the company. Nox could understand that. It was pretty lonely being lost.

Well, it wasn't long before they were back in scum-filled territory. They spotted a ramshackle settlement ahead, and they didn't quite know the place until they saw the weathered sign: *Oldtown*.

Nox raised an eyebrow and cast a knowing glance at Oakley.

They'd barely stepped foot inside the settlement when they were accosted by a posse led by Ben Budson, the mayor of Oldtown. Old Reliable was his horse once, and Chance Oakley'd made away with him without paying. Budson was a cruel man, but he was crueller to animals more than men. You see, animals didn't have guns.

"I told ya we'd be back for ya," Budson hollered.

"Funny, that," Nox said. "Seems we're back for

you."

"Ain't nothin' funny 'bout a sheriff who breaks the law." Budson looked over his shoulder to his comrades. "That's the kind of thing that deserves some broken legs, don't you think, fellas?"

"It's been more than a week," Nox said, referencing Budson's prior promise. Many "brave" men made promises like that in the moment, more to ease their hurt prides and make a show in front of their posse than anything else. Few lived up to them. You see, you had to be a man of your word to honour a promise.

"Let's consider that a generosity," Budson said.

"Yeah," Nox replied, clicking back the hammer on his revolver. "Let's."

"Now, there's no cause for fightin'," Oakley said. He didn't pull out his rifle. He wasn't fast on the draw like the rest of them. He thought drawing at all would just be salting wounds, and maybe opening new ones.

"Oh, you're one to talk 'bout *no cause*," Budson said. "You think you can cross me and get away with it? This is the Wild North, God damn it!"

Nox felt a kind of ease he hadn't felt in a while. Yeah, they were back in familiar sands alright. The uncertainty of the Lostlands was gone. It was back to the draw, back to the shootouts, back to the common gangs and criminals. You know, the little things in life.

"Here," Nox said, reaching into his pocket and casting a bag of coils into the air. He did it with such speed that they thought he was drawing another weapon. They fired at the bag, letting the coils scatter. "What?" Nox said as they landed. "You don't want it now?"

"You're weeks too late," Budson said.

"So are you, but hey, don't you know I've been busy?"

"You got your money now," Oakley said. "Let's all just walk away."

Budson's eyes were full of rage. "Do you think I'm gonna crawl on the ground for your iron, Coilhunter?"

"Better than lead," Nox rasped. He gave a little twist of his revolver to draw their attention to it. They remembered when he'd disarmed the lot of them with one quick fan of the hammer. Some of them were still wearing bandages on their hands. Some of them were pointing pistols with what wasn't their gun hand.

"Hand 'im over, Coilhunter," Budson said. "This is the frontiers. He deserves frontier justice."

"I deserve a second chance," Oakley said. "Lord, I've given out enough of 'em. And Old Reliable here deserved a second chance too, a chance with someone who'd look after him, treat him proper."

Budson scoffed. "Treat 'im proper? What in God's name did ya do to his legs?"

"The land did that," Nox said.

"Well, the land didn't do what's gonna happen next."

"No," Nox said. "I did."

He swapped revolvers, just to show them he was fast enough to do it, and fanned the hammer as he pinged those pistols right out of their hands. They all had two hands, and that was a wound to each on separate occasions. You'd think they didn't want to hold a pistol at all.

"Let. It. Go," Nox barked.

But he knew Budson wouldn't let it go, so he stomped on up to him, whacked him in the face with his mask, just enough to disorient him, and hauled him up over his shoulder. He carried him over to his monowheel and dropped him in the bounty box at the back.

"There," Nox said. "Is this what you want? This is where folk like you end up. This is the end of the path you're clamourin' for. Now, I gave you a way out. The only other way for you is a life of crime. I can see it in your eyes. You're gonna go on from town to town with vendettas, with grudges, with a need to right unrightable wrongs. And I get it. I truly do. But you're startin' to cross the line. *My* line. I can almost see your face on the wall already. You're lost. Well, let me help you find yourself."

Budson said nothing. He was caught up in the moment, staring at Nox with a kind of terror in his eyes. Oh, he thought he was a strong man, a man who'd take nothing from no one, not even the Coilhunter. But here he was, taking it all the same. He was lucky he wasn't taking bullets too.

"Is this what you want?" Nox repeated. "'Cause I can finish this now. You're already almost at the end."

"Please!" Budson whimpered. Oh, how they all whimpered. Even did it while drawing the gun. Sometimes it was good to let them whimper, and let them live. When other grim folk saw those whimpers, then maybe they'd think twice. You see, mercy was a weapon too.

Budson clambered out of the box, picked up what

coils he could, and ran. He should've kept looking ahead, or looking down at the pouch in his hands, but he looked back. That told them enough.

"He's not gonna let this go," Oakley said.

Nox sighed. "Well, he's had his warnin'. Let's call this his second chance."

They shared a drink at the local rum-hole, and told themselves their throats deserved a second chance as well. After a few more whiskeys, and a few more tales, they decided to call it a night, and call a night on this whole chapter of their lives.

"Well, thanks for everything, Nathaniel," Oakley said. "You don't know how much it means to me. Just shows me I've found me a true friend out there after all. Not got many of those, mind. But few and true is better than lots and false, as they say. Guess I ain't too old to learn somethin'. And if there's somethin' I've learned in life, it's this: You can't just be a spectator on someone else's path. You've gotta walk your own."

The Coilhunter nodded to him. "Well, ain't that the truth. All the best, Chance, with wherever the wind takes you."

Oakley tipped his hat. "Same to you, drifter."

As Oakley trotted off, and Old Reliable gave a friendly whinny, Nox couldn't help but feel a pang of sadness. He knew he couldn't afford friends. No amount of coils could pay for those. You see, the life he chose, or the life that'd been forced on him, was a lonely one. Others'd just get in the way. In the way of the hunt. In the way of the bullets. He was already carrying a lot. He couldn't carry the weight of their deaths as well.

The truth of it, he knew, was that he was a Lostlander too. No, the Northfolk didn't call him that. That wasn't one of his thousand names. But it was how he felt, beneath the layers of the gunslinger and the bounty hunter, beneath the hardened shell of his heart. He'd lost so much, and no amount of searching would help him find it. Even when he'd found the killers, he hadn't found peace. No, he had to remain lost. He had to keep roaming, keep drifting. He had to keep hunting. He had to go on. Some said that, like the desert, he'd go on forever.

ABOUT THE AUTHOR

Dean F. Wilson was born in Dublin, Ireland in 1987. He started writing at age 11, and has since become a *USA Today* and *Wall Street Journal* Bestselling Author.

He is the author of the *Children of Telm* epic fantasy trilogy, the *Great Iron War* steampunk series, the *Coilhunter Chronicles* science-fiction western series, the *Hibernian Hollows* urban fantasy series, and the *Infinite Stars* space opera series.

Dean previously worked as a journalist, primarily in the field of technology. He has written for *TechEye*, *Thinq*, *V3*, *VR-Zone*, *ITProPortal*, *TechRadar Pro*, and *The Inquirer*.

www.deanfwilson.com